GIFT OF THE WITCH

A WITCHES OF KEATING HOLLOW NOVELLA

KEATING HOLLOW HAPPILY EVER AFTERS
BOOK ONE

DEANNA CHASE

Bayou Moon Press, LLC

www.deannachase.com

Printed in the United States of America

ABOUT THIS BOOK

Clay Garrison is having a bad week. The newest
batches of beer at the Townsend Brewery have been
corrupted. Luckily, his earth witch wife, Abby, has been
testing her own brews. Now it's up to her batches to
save the summer season's profits. The problem?
Everything is going wrong, and when a dire warning
comes from the ghost of an old friend, Abby is starting
to believe someone, or something, is out to get them.
She'll need her witchy powers to save the day and, in
the end, reveal the gift of the witch.

CHAPTER 1

"With the power of the moon and stars, let this potion be a slumber charm," Abby Garrison said as magic sparked from her fingertips and onto the wooden spoon she used to stir her potion. The thin, herb-infused liquid in her copper pot went from a pale green to a deep midnight blue. She smiled down at her creation, pleased with herself. Her newly developed sleep potion had worked perfectly.

"Abby!" The door to her studio swung open and in walked her husband, Clay Garrison.

"Clay? What are you doing here?" Abby put her wooden spoon down and wiped her hands on her apron, frowning in confusion. "Aren't you supposed to be bottling today?"

Her husband was the brewmaster at her family's brewery in town. The fact he'd come all the way out to her father's property, where Abby made her magical potions and soaps, was highly unusual. "I was, but there's a major problem with my tanks. I need you to come down to the brewery so we can test your batches. If they aren't ready, we're going to have a major problem supplying our vendors with product."

"I was going to give them at least another week," she said, already untying her apron. "What happened? Are all of your batches ruined?"

"All of them." He held the door open for her and followed her out.

Abby stopped in her tracks and turned to her husband, taking in the worry lines around his eyes. She pressed one hand to his chest and the other to his cheek. "Clay? What happened to the tanks?"

He ground his teeth together and closed his eyes as he nodded. "One of the new ones imploded and ruined the other four. We're going to have to replace them all."

Abby's heart sank all the way to her toes as her limbs went cold. "No," she whispered, fearing the worst. "Was anyone hurt?"

His eyes flew open and he quickly shook his head. "No. No one was in the brewhouse when it happened. Thank the gods."

"But what about replacing the tanks? Dad doesn't

have that kind of money just lying around." Her heart was nearly beating out of her chest now. Her father owned the brewery, and while they made a good living, it would cost over six figures to replace what had been lost.

He covered her hand that was still cupping his cheek and then brought it to his lips to kiss it gently. "Don't worry, Abs. Insurance will cover the damage. Our biggest problem now is having product to supply to our accounts. That's why we need to go test your experiments. If it looks promising, we need to get started on the marketing and notifications of a change in our lineup."

"That's a lot of pressure," she said, falling into step beside him. The batches in the backup tanks were her first try at brewing beer. Sure, she'd learned a lot, growing up as a brewmaster's daughter, but watching and learning wasn't the same as doing. "My batches could be terrible."

Clay grabbed her hand and squeezed. "They could," he agreed. "They could also be delicious. We just won't know until we try."

She sucked in a deep breath. "And if they are terrible? What then?"

"Then we'll be behind for at least a month and the business will take a pretty significant financial hit. But we'll get through it."

Abby eyed him and frowned. "The brewery isn't in the position to lose a month's worth of income right now. Not after the new roof and the upgrades to the tanks we did this year. Plus, production will be limited if we're just using the backup tanks until the others are replaced. That sounds more like two months behind."

A muscle ticked in Clay's jaw. "I know, but we'll find a way to work it out."

She nodded and paused at the back door of her childhood home. "Hold on, we need to let Clair know where I'll be."

Clay opened the back door to her father's house, and the two of them walked in together.

"Hey there, sweetheart," Clay said, striding across the living room and picking up their two-year-old who'd been playing on a blanket with her pile of stuffed animals.

Lynette squealed as her father picked her up and spun her around the way he always did when he got home from work.

"Well, this is a surprise," Clair said, rising from her spot on the couch. "What brings you out here in the middle of the day, Clay?"

He gave her a quick smile. "Just came to grab Abby. I need her for a couple of hours at the brewery."

Abby moved to stand next to Clair, her father's longtime partner. She'd graciously offered to watch

Lynette a few times a week so that Abby could spend time in her potion studio, keeping up with her online business. "Do you mind watching our girl for a few more hours?"

"Not at all." Clair gave Abby a warm smile. "I can't think of a better way to spend my afternoon."

Abby chuckled. "I don't know. The spa sounds pretty appealing to me. Especially after Endora nearly ripped my arm out of the socket on our walk yesterday," Abby said, referring to their fourteen-year-old daughter's rambunctious golden retriever. "Usually Olive walks her, but she had to finish a school project."

Clair's face softened as she watched Lynette and Clay. "Spa appointments are great and all, but they don't hold a candle to spending time with your little cutie."

"I think my heart just exploded," Abby said, clutching her chest. Then she took a step forward and wrapped Clair in a hug. "You're the best. You know that, right?"

"I do," she said with a chuckle and then stepped back.

Clay gave Lynette a kiss on her cheek and then placed the toddler back on the floor. He knelt down so he was at eye level with his daughter. "You have fun with Grandma Clair. Mommy and I will see you in a few hours."

The toddler hugged him and then ran over to Clair and wrapped her arms around the older woman's right leg, leaning in as if claiming her.

Clair beamed down at the little girl, and Abby wished her dad would go ahead and ask Clair to marry him already. The couple had been dating for two decades. While she understood his reluctance to get remarried after his trauma of being abandoned by her mother, there was no indication that Clair was ever leaving the family.

Abby's heart was so full, she thought it might burst. Whatever was happening at the brewery, they'd get through it. She knew that. This right here, their daughter and family, were what was most important. Kneeling in front of her daughter, Abby gave her kisses and then squeezed Clair's hand before she followed her husband out of the house.

Clay walked to his truck and opened the passenger door. "I'll bring you back later for your SUV."

She nodded and climbed into the new truck they'd purchased just last year. It had come in useful since he was attending more beer festivals, while Abby had taken on a booth at the weekly farmer's market in the middle of town.

"You know," Clay said, glancing over at her as he made the way down the long treelined driveway, "I thought for sure your dad was going to propose to Clair last month on Valentine's Day."

"You did?" Abby asked, surprised. "Why?"

"He was asking me about what I thought of his plans. If it was romantic enough." Clay chuckled. "He wanted to take her to the beach, but I told him that being bundled up from the wind and cold in the middle of February on the northern California coast didn't sound all that romantic. I told him to book a cabin that overlooked the coast and to plan a romantic candlelit dinner with a fire in the fireplace."

Abby frowned and pressed her hand to her churning gut as she feared she'd been the one who messed up her dad's plans. "They didn't go away for Valentine's Day. They watched Lynette and Olive."

He nodded. "I know. I tried to tell them it wasn't necessary, that we were happy to spend the night with them, but Clair wasn't having it. She said it was exactly how she wanted to spend the evening. When I asked your dad about it, he said it wasn't a problem. That they'd delayed their getaway due to other reasons. I never did find out what happened."

"That was a month ago," Abby said, frowning. "They haven't gone anywhere and as far as I know, they don't have any plans to do so. I wonder if Dad got cold feet." Abby made a mental note to ask her dad about it. She knew nothing would mean more to Clair than to officially be part of the family.

"Maybe he did." Clay reached over and squeezed his wife's hand. "Lin Townsend doesn't really seem like the type of man who gets cold feet though."

Abby blew out a breath. "I don't know, Clay. Normally I'd say you're right. He's been the rock of this family. Unafraid of anything. But he's been so gun shy about remarrying, it's possible."

Clay pulled the truck into the parking lot of the Keating Hollow Brewery and jumped out. A moment later he was pulling Abby's door open and helping her out of the vehicle.

"Thank you," Abby said, smiling softly at her husband. They'd been married for four years and, as her sisters would say, the honeymoon stage had never ended. In fact, Abby was more in love with Clay and their two daughters every day.

He took a moment to wrap his arms around her and kiss her so thoroughly that when someone cleared their throat, it took her a moment to even realize they weren't alone.

"You do know this is a parking lot and not your bedroom, right?" she heard her father ask, his tone teasing.

Abby disentangled herself from her husband and glanced around him at Lincoln Townsend. Her father was standing near the front of their truck, his arms crossed over his chest, looking amused, if not a little impatient. "Hi, Dad. Sorry."

"I'm not," Clay said with a chuckle, placing his hand on the small of her back. "Getting my wife alone without any kids is damn near impossible these days. I'd be a fool if I didn't take advantage of the situation." He winked at Abby.

Lin let out a groan. "You do realize I'm her father, right?"

Clay just shrugged. "You have a two-year-old granddaughter. I imagine you know where she came from."

"Okay. That's enough," Lin said with a chuckle and a shake of his head. "We have some beer to test. That is why you brought my daughter here, right?"

"Right." Abby slipped her arm through her father's and walked with him toward the old brewhouse where the backup tanks were housed.

CHAPTER 2

"*D*ad, when are you taking Clair out of town?" Abby asked as they walked across the property.

He glanced down at her, his eyes narrowed in curiosity. "Why do you think I'm taking Clair out of town?"

Abby cleared her throat. "Well, Clay said you were talking about taking her to the beach. You know, a romantic getaway. I bet she'd love that."

Her father stiffened and his gait faltered for just a second before he recovered and kept moving forward.

"Dad?"

"What Abby?" His tone held a slight warning.

She knew she should drop the subject, but after what Clay had told her in the truck, she just couldn't let this go. She paused at the door to the old brewhouse and turned to her dad. "What are you waiting for? I know Clair loves you. She loves our entire family. Isn't it time you two made it official?"

"Abby, this isn't any of your business," he said with a finality that indicated he wasn't going to talk about the subject with her.

Still, she pressed. "You don't think so? She's taken on the role of grandmother. The role my own mother is uncapable of embracing. Not that I'd let her around the kids anyway." Abby's mother was a potions addict. And even though she claimed to be sober, Abby had reasons to believe her mother wasn't being truthful with her. "Faith, Yvette, Noel, and I see her as a mother. You know that, right?"

He nodded as he shoved his hands into his jean's pockets. "You know she loves filling that place in all your lives. And your kids' lives, too. What difference does it make if a piece of paper says we're married? She's already part of the family."

Abby couldn't deny his argument. "That's true. I just think it would mean a lot to her if she was officially a Townsend." She bit down on her bottom lip, contemplating if she should continue. Then the words just came flying out of her mouth. "I know it would mean a lot to me."

Lincoln Townsend grimaced and pulled the door to

the brewhouse open. "This conversation is over, Abby. I won't be shamed into a decision like this."

"Dad! That's not—" The door slammed in her face and she took a step back, her own grimace claiming her lips.

"That went well," Clay said, going heavy on the sarcasm.

Abby turned to her husband, red-faced, and pressed her cheek to his shoulder. "Ugh. That is not how I envisioned that going."

He ran his fingers down her spine and kissed the top of her head. "I know. Maybe now that you planted the seed, he'll think more about it."

She pulled back and stared up at him, her stomach churning with anxiety. "Or he'll never do it just to spite me and I'll have ruined it for Clair forever."

Clay reached up and brushed a lock of her long blond hair out of her eyes. "You didn't ruin anything. He loves Clair, and she loves him and the rest of you. It's going to be okay."

Abby blew out a frustrated breath. "I just want the best for both of them."

"I know, love." He gave her a quick hug and then reached past her to pull the door open. "Come on. Let's check out your first batches of beer and see if we're going to be bottling the rest of the week."

Groaning to herself, certain that now that they

needed her batches they'd turn out to be a total loss, she followed Clay into the building and prayed her father wasn't too upset with her after she'd questioned him about Clair.

"Clay," Lincoln called from the other side of the room. "Clear your schedule for the weekend. We just put the Fortuna Beer Festival back on the calendar."

Abby let out a small gasp. "Does that mean my batches are decent?"

"Better than decent, Abigail," her father said, appearing right before her, his face beaming with pride. "These batches are going to win awards."

"You're getting a little carried away, don't you think?" Abby asked him. "Come on, Dad. Don't let your judgment be clouded just because I made those batches."

Her father let out a low chuckle. "Honey, there isn't anything wrong with my judgment." He turned and beckoned to Clay. "Come on, son. Prepare to be amazed."

Clay raised both eyebrows at Abby, gave her an amused smile, and followed her father.

Abby hurried to keep up with her husband's long strides.

When they reached Lin, he already had samples waiting for them. "Who would've thought something we're calling French Toast Porter would be winning blue ribbons?"

"Dad." Abby rolled her eyes, certain that her father was exaggerating. There was no way her first try as a brewer was going to win the brewery awards.

"I'm telling you, Abby. This is one we're going to want to put on the regular menu." He handed Clay and Abby each a plastic cup that was about a quarter full. "Try it and then tell me we don't have a winner on our hands."

Abby held her cup, but didn't make a move to taste it. She was too busy studying Clay to see how he really felt about the French Toast Porter she'd concocted.

Clay held the cup up, eyeing the color of the rich brown liquid. He then put the cup to his nose and deeply inhaled. His eyes closed and his lips curved into a small smile. "The aroma is pretty heady. Sweet, a little nutty with a hint of spice."

Lincoln nodded. "Yes, the aroma is wonderful, too."

Abby clutched her cup, but still made no move to try the beer. Instead, she kept her gaze locked on her husband as he tipped the cup back and took a large sip of the beer.

His eyes closed again as he held the liquid on his tongue, and when he finally swallowed, his shoulders relaxed and a huge grin spread across his handsome face. "Damn, Abs," he said softly. "Are you trying to come for my job? This is incredible."

Abby beamed at both her husband and her father. "It's really that good?"

"It's really that good." Her father patted her on the shoulder. "Try it. See for yourself. Clay and I are going to test the Caramel Apple Blond Ale and the Cheesecake Chocolate Stout."

"If they are even half as good as this porter, we're in for a very good summer," Clay said as the two of them headed back to the tanks to draw more samples.

Abby's stomach fluttered with excitement as she held the beer up to her own nose. The rich aroma reminded her of weekend mornings when she'd stayed the night at her best friend Charlotte's house. Mary Pelsh, Charlotte's mother, always made them French toast. And it was always divine. Abby could still taste the real maple syrup, the dash of cinnamon, and the thick homemade Challah bread. That was the combination she'd been going for when she'd mixed up the batch of ingredients for the porter. It was also what she'd focused on while mixing the batch before turning it loose to ferment.

Standing there in the brewhouse, Abby brought the cup up to her lips, but just as she was about to taste the beer she'd been waiting to try for the last two months, a slightly warm breeze washed over her, and her arm was suddenly jolted, causing the plastic cup to slip from her fingertips. The cup hit the pristine cement floor, and the beer splattered, ruining her chance to taste the brew both her father and her husband had been raving about.

"Dammit," she muttered, kneeling down to pick up the cup. From the corner of her eye, she spotted movement and froze when her gaze landed on the brown-skinned young woman hovering near the open door. "Charlotte?" she whispered in amazement.

Her friend, who'd died when they were high school seniors, was forever suspended in time at the age of eighteen. She winked at Abby just before she floated outside into the afternoon sun.

Abby quickly stood and then wobbled when her head swam from the sudden movement. She reached out to steady herself and then carefully made her way to the still-open door. When she peeked out at the area behind the brewery, all she saw were redwoods and blue skies. She blinked and took another look, desperately wishing her best friend would make another appearance. When she was sure Charlotte was gone for good, she reluctantly turned around and headed back into the brewhouse to look for her father and husband.

"The French Toast gets my vote to be entered into the contest, but the other two are also strong contenders," Clay said, waving at the empty beer cups in front of him.

"I think we might have a better chance at a ribbon if we enter the Cheesecake Chocolate Stout," her father said thoughtfully. "It's usually an under represented category."

Abby raised her eyebrows. "Are you two seriously debating which of my beers to enter into the contest at the beer festival this weekend?"

"Yes," her father said with a quick nod. "We were going to go with both, but there's another festival at the end of the month that usually gets better press coverage. We don't want to spoil the element of surprise. I think the stout this weekend, but Clay is sold on the porter. And we need to decide by this afternoon so Clay can send in the entry before the deadline."

"Does that mean I'm the tie breaker?" Abby asked, eyeing the empty cups.

Clay chuckled. "I guess so. Let me—" He was cut off when Abby's watch alarm started to go off.

"Too late," Abby said, silencing the alarm. "I've got to go and pick up Olive from her piano lessons. I guess you two will have to play rock, paper, scissors or something to decide the outcome." She rummaged around in her bag, searching for her keys, but then stopped suddenly, realizing she'd left them in her studio. " Clay, I need your keys. Mine are sitting on the side table in my shed."

"Sure." He pulled out his key chain, the red crystal Olive had given him recently, glinting in the afternoon sunlight. "Thanks." She turned to her father. "Dad, can you give Clay a lift back to your house when you're done so he can grab my keys and then pick up Lynette and my SUV?"

"Sure, honey," Lin said.

She kissed her father's cheek and then her husband's before turning to leave the brewhouse.

"Abs?" Clay called after her.

"Yeah?" she said, pausing at the door.

"Good work, babe. Your brews are going to save us this summer."

Her father nodded his agreement.

She grinned. "I'm just happy I produced something drinkable."

"It's way better than drinkable," her father confirmed. "In fact, we're going to need you to start another batch at the end of the week. Can you do that?"

"Sure." She waved a hand at them and took off for Clay's truck.

CHAPTER 3

"*H*ow was practice?" Abby asked Olive as the fourteen-year-old climbed into the truck.

"It was great. Chad said I might be a prodigy." She clipped her seatbelt together and turned to Abby, her eyes dancing with excitement. "There's a competition at Humboldt State next month that he wants me to enter."

"That's amazing, honey," Abby said, trying to stay focused on her stepdaughter. Between her intermittent nausea and the fact that she couldn't stop thinking about seeing Charlotte's ghost, Abby was a lot more distracted than usual.

"I'm just not sure if I'm ready," Olive said, worrying her bottom lip with her teeth.

"I'm sure if Chad thinks you are, then you should

give it a go." Chad Garber was her sister Hope's husband, and prior to opening his music store in Keating Hollow, he'd been a professional concert pianist.

"That's what Aunt Hope said. I'm just... I don't know, kinda nervous, I guess. I never thought I'd be entering competitions. I just took lessons because it sounded cool."

"Are you sure it's not because Jack Jensen signed up for lessons?" Abby teased.

Olive's face flushed red as she turned to stare out the window. She cleared her throat. "No. Why would you say that?"

Abby winced, silently berating herself for letting that comment fly. She knew that Olive had a crush on the young man who'd moved to Keating Hollow last fall. It wasn't long after they'd learned that he was taking private lessons with Chad that Olive had suddenly developed an interest in piano. Abby debated what to say, then decided to just be honest with the young teenager. It was better to know she could talk to Abby, right? She sure hoped so. "I didn't mean to embarrass you, Olive," she said gently.

"I'm not embarrassed," Olive insisted, twisting back around to stare at Abby. "I just don't know why you think that."

Abby pulled the truck into the driveway in front of

their house and put the vehicle in Park. Olive immediately reached for the door handle, but before she could jump out and disappear into her bedroom, Abby put her hand on the girl's arm. "I just want you to know I'm here if you want to talk."

"About what?" Olive gave her stepmother a defiant look. and Abby couldn't deny that she might deserve it.

"You know. Boys. Dating. Teenager stuff."

"Just boys?" Olive asked with a disapproving cluck of her tongue. "What if I want to date girls? That's pretty bold of you to assume I'd just date guys, don't you think? What's next? An arranged marriage?"

The teenage sarcasm was strong, and all Abby could do was laugh at herself. She chuckled softly. "I'm botching this badly, aren't I?"

Abby expected Olive to react with either an eyeroll or a chuckle. What she didn't expect was the apprehensive expression that flashed in her daughter's eyes before she glanced away again.

"Olive," Abby said gently, suddenly terrified that Olive was trying to tell her something about her sexuality and she'd completely missed it, thinking the girl was just being contrary. "You do know that your father and I love you no matter who you date, right? There's no judgment here. Only acceptance. Understand?"

Her stepdaughter turned to her with a serious

expression and nodded. "I do. I'm not... I don't..." She wrinkled her nose.

"It's okay, Olive. Whatever it is, you can tell me." Was this the moment her stepdaughter would tell her something life changing? Why wasn't Clay here? She said a silent prayer to the goddess that she was handling this correctly.

Olive blew out a long breath and finally looked Abby in the eye. "If I were to date anyone, I think it would be a boy."

"Oh. Okay." Abby frowned, trying to understand what had just happened.

Olive sat back in her seat, her eyes closed as she said, "One of my friends at school likes girls."

There it was. Now Abby understood. Olive wanted to prove the point that no one should make assumptions and she likely wanted to make sure her parents weren't going to judge her friend.

"Does she like anyone in particular?" Abby asked, trying to show that there was no reason to be worried about talking about this topic.

Olive shrugged. "Honestly, I'm not really sure."

There was a weird tension in the air after such an important subject. Abby needed to shift the vibe, and if there was one thing she could count on, it was that Olive would always laugh at her stepmother when she owned her awkward blundering. "Did I ever tell you about the first time I noticed your dad?"

"Uh, no."

Abby gave her a sheepish smile. "I knew him of course. Growing up in the same small town, that's to be expected. But the first time I knew I *liked* him, I think I was just about your age. My friend Charlotte dared me to ask him to eat lunch together."

"Did you?"

"Of course. A girl never turns down a double-dog-dare challenge," Abby said, sounding indignant.

Olive giggled. "No. I'd imagine she wouldn't."

"So I asked him to have lunch with me on pizza day, and he did. Neither of us said anything, and then after ten minutes, he jumped up and said he had to get to class. I was pretty proud of myself and was beaming when I strode back over to Charlotte, ready to brag about how I'd just had the best date. Then Charlotte pointed at my mouth and said I had green stuff on my teeth."

Olive's eyes widened. "You did?"

Abby nodded solemnly. "Yep. There was a giant piece of pepper stuff right here." She indicated the space between her two front teeth. "Then when I went to get it out, I saw I had a zit forming on my nose. I actually wished for the ground to open up and swallow me whole."

"It's amazing he married you even all those years later," Olive said with a giggle.

"Right? That's how we know he's a good man." Abby ruffled Olive's hair. "Now come on. Let's get inside and start working on dinner."

Olive was still laughing as she jumped out of the truck and ran into the house.

Abby followed, moving slower than usual. Her stomach was still unsettled, and she was just more fatigued than normal. "Please don't let me be coming down with something," she said to herself as she followed Olive into the house.

Endora, the most rambunctious golden retriever ever, ran flat out toward Abby the second she walked through the door. The dog jumped up, pawing at Abby and smearing slobber all over her shirt.

"Endora!" Olive called. "Get down. It's time for dinner."

The dog instantly shot toward Olive and raced into the kitchen.

Abby looked down at herself and sighed. "Olive, I'm going to jump into the shower. I'll be out in a few minutes."

"Okay," Olive called back.

Abby pressed her hand to her stomach, trying to calm her churning gut, and disappeared into the primary bedroom she shared with Clay.

Once she was under the hot spray, she stood there for far too long, letting the water run over her, just breathing. Her life was hectic with a husband and two kids, one of which was a toddler, as well as a career to manage. But she wouldn't change it for anything. She loved her life. She just wished there were more hours in the day so that she had a little more down time to herself.

When she finally emerged from the bedroom, dressed in sweats and an oversized sweatshirt, the scent of garlic and onions overwhelmed her and nearly made her bolt for the bathroom. Instead, she held herself up against the wall and breathed until the nausea passed.

The sound of the door opening had Abby moving toward the living room. "Clay?" she called.

"In here."

She followed his voice and found him and her father standing in her living room. Abby frowned. "Didn't you go get Lynette and my car?"

"Your car and our child are already here." He nodded toward the kitchen.

Abby turned and spotted Olive holding her little sister at the table while Clair was busy working on dinner. "Oh wow." She walked over and leaned against Clay. "I was in the shower and apparently missed some details."

"Abby, you look so pale. Take a seat. I've got this," Clair said. "The spaghetti will be done in no time."

"Clair, you've done so much already. You don't need to make dinner for us, too." Abby tried to leave Clay's side, but he tightened his arm around her shoulder, holding her in place.

"She's right," Clay said, his face full of concern. "You do look pale. Come on. You sit and I'll take over in the kitchen."

Abby let him lead her to the couch. Once she was curled up in the corner, he retreated to the kitchen and ordered Clair to join Abby.

Clair made a few protests, but when Lincoln chimed in to back up Clay's orders, she threw her hands up and said, "Fine. Fine. I'll go chat with Abby."

"You're too good to us," Abby said to Clair when the woman took a seat next to her on the couch.

"You know I'm happy to do it." Clair squeezed Abby's hand. "You know I never had kids of my own, but I have been an excellent aunt. And now a grandmother of sorts."

"There is no 'of sorts' about it, Clair." Abby held her gaze, trying to convey just how much her father's girlfriend meant to her and her family. "You are their grandma. Just like Clay's mom is. Don't you dare ever doubt that. Okay?"

Clair's hazel eyes glittered with tears as she gave

Abby a shaky smile. "Thank you, Abby. You know you all mean the world to me."

"You're the mother I never had," Abby choked out. "We all feel that way."

One tear slid down Clair's cheek, but she didn't bother to brush it away. Instead, she reached over and gave Abby a long hug. "Thank you, sweetie."

"Thank you," Abby said into her long auburn hair.

"Abby?" her father said as he crossed the room, holding a glass. "We brought a growler of the porter home. Did you want to try it now?"

She glanced up at her father. He was holding a beer glass filled with the rich brown liquid. "Oh, Dad, I would, but my stomach isn't quite right. I think I'll wait until tomorrow when I'm feeling a little better."

Her dad's expression turned worried. "Are you coming down with the stomach flu?"

"I don't know to be honest. The symptoms just started."

"Lynette doesn't seem to be sick. Looks like Olive is okay, too," Clair said, eyeing the girls, who were still at the table. Olive was braiding Lynette's hair while the toddler petted the golden retriever who sat perfectly still, letting Lynette do whatever she wanted.

"I swear, that dog only behaves for Lynette," Abby said with a small shake of her head.

"It's remarkable that such a high-energy dog can sit that long for her," Clair mused.

"It is." Abby sat back and smiled tiredly at her family.

"Here," Clay said, walking over and handing her a ginger ale. "Maybe this will help."

"Thanks." She gave her husband a grateful glance.

Clair stood and walked over to the mantle over the fireplace. She picked up a silver-framed photo of Abby and Clay that was taken only two months ago when they'd slipped away for an overnight by themselves at the coast. She held it up as she turned to Abby. "This is new, isn't it?"

"It is. I just put it out last week."

Clair gave a wistful sigh. "Lincoln and I had plans to go to the coast for Valentine's Day, but we had a scheduling conflict. I'm hoping we can reschedule soon."

Abby sat up. "You should do it. Book for the spring Solstice. You know, celebrate new beginnings and all that."

"Yeah. That would be nice," Clair said as she gently put the framed picture back down. "I'm not sure about Lincoln's schedule though."

"My schedule?" Abby's father asked as he appeared in the living room again. "What about it? Things are crazy right now due to the tank situation, but if there's something you need me to do, I can try to fit it in."

Clair shook her head. "It's nothing. Really."

"No it isn't," Abby said, her temper flaring at the fact that her father seemed to be putting Clair off. "You need to reschedule that trip to the coast with Clair, Dad. I was saying you should do it on the Solstice. It's the perfect—"

"That's only a week and a half away, Abby," her father said sternly. "You know I can't do that. Not now. There's too much to do."

"Clay and I can cover it," she said stubbornly.

"Abby," her father warned. "Drop it. Clair and I will reschedule when it's convenient for us." He walked over to his girlfriend and held out his hand. "Ready to go?"

"I thought you were staying for dinner," Abby said, alarmed that she'd offended her father.

"We have other plans," her father said.

"But Clair was making dinner. I thought—"

"It's okay, Abby," Clair said, patting her shoulder. "You're not feeling well. I was just trying to help by starting dinner for you since you were in the shower. I'll see you Thursday?"

That was the next day that Clair had offered to watch Lynette while Abby worked in her studio. "Yeah. Okay. Thanks for everything." She pushed herself to her feet and walked over to her father. "Dad, I'm sorry if I overstepped."

Her father's expression softened, and he gave her a quick kiss on the cheek. "Don't worry about it, Abigail. Go relax with your family. We'll talk later."

Abby stood at the door, watching as her father and Clair climbed into his SUV and drove off down their residential street. After she closed the door, she turned around and spotted the glass of beer her father had left on the coffee table. She reached down to grab it, but just as her hand closed around the glass, Endora bounded up to her, knocking the glass out of her hand.

"Dammit!" Abby said, watching as the beer ran over her coffee table and down onto the rug that covered the hardwood floor. "That's twice today!" She hurried to grab a towel to clean up, and when she was finished, she glanced up and could have sworn she spotted her friend Charlotte watching her. But when she blinked, the ghostly figure was gone again.

Abby sat back on her heels, her palm pressed to her chest as her heart raced. There was no doubt about it. Her best friend was back, and Abby was determined to find out why.

CHAPTER 4

*A*bby woke the next day with only one thing on her mind.

Charlotte.

In fact, she had a sneaky feeling that she'd dreamed about her friend because she had a vague contented feeling that she usually experienced after a girls' night.

The bed dipped, and Abby turned to find Clay sitting next to her. "How are you feeling this morning?"

"Better," she said, hoping that was true. The night before she'd spent an hour or two gagging up bile. She hadn't been able to eat, and when she'd lost the battle with her stomach, she'd spent some time hovering over the commode, much to her dismay.

"I'm going to take Lynette over to the spa and give

you a break today," he said, pushing her hair out of her eyes.

"The spa? What is she doing? Getting a massage?"

He laughed. "I don't know. Is that what Faith's triplets do there?"

Abby chuckled softly. "No. I think they run around, fighting over half a dozen stuffed animals and drive the nanny crazy. Lynette will love it."

Clay pressed the back of his hand to her forehead and then pursed his lips. "You don't seem like you have a fever. Just a twenty-four-hour bug?"

She brushed his hand aside and pushed herself up to lean against the headboard. "I certainly hope so. You don't have to take Lynette. I'm sure we'll be good here."

"Nah. She's already excited to see her cousins, and Faith said it's no problem to bring her by. I don't want to disappoint her. Just take the day to do whatever you want. The rest of the week will be pretty busy."

"It will?" she asked, her brain not quite keeping up.

"Aren't you working at your studio tomorrow?"

"Sure. But I always do that on Thursdays."

He nodded. "And Friday we need you at the brewery to start another batch of your beer creations."

Abby nodded. "Right. I forgot about that." Then her heart was a little heavy when she realized she wouldn't be spending Friday with her daughter. That was normally her favorite day of the week, when she took

Lynette to the park or on a golf cart ride or even just to Incantation Café where she'd meet with Wanda and have cookies and hot chocolate. It was time that was special to Abby. "We'll need to find a sitter for Lynette."

"I'll ask Faith when I drop her off today. If that doesn't work, I'll check in with Noel."

"It's a good thing I have a big family," Abby said half-heartedly.

"Tell me how you really feel," her husband said and then kissed her softly. "Take the day to rest and recover. My mom is going to pick up Olive and Lynette this afternoon. So don't worry about a thing."

"Sounds good. Thank her for me." Abby grabbed his hand and tugged him down for another kiss. When she pulled away, she remembered that he was going to start bottling that day and that the insurance adjuster was scheduled to come inspect the bad tanks. She craned her neck to stare up at him. "Good luck today."

"Thanks. We're going to need it." He slipped out of the room, and before she even made it out of her bathroom, she heard the front door close and the voices of her family outside as they climbed into his truck.

It was odd to be the only person in her house. Abby couldn't remember a time in recent memory when she didn't have at least Lynette around. If it hadn't been for Endora pawing at her foot for a treat, she was certain she'd have almost felt lonely. "Hold on, Ms. Impatient," Abby said to the dog. "I'll get it for you."

The dog spun around a few times like she was possessed, but the minute Abby fished the treat out of the bag, Endora sat her butt on the floor and waited patiently for Abby to offer her the treat.

"You're something else, you know that, right?" She gave the dog the treat and watched as she ran off to her bed in the corner of the living room where she could savor her prize.

Abby turned her attention to the kitchen, intending to make coffee, but as soon as she opened the container, the scent of the fresh grounds overwhelmed her and made her stomach roll again. She quickly closed the bag and stuffed it back in the cabinet. She stood at the counter, her hands on the cool surface as she waited for the nausea to pass... again.

"Damn," she whispered and went to the fridge to grab a ginger ale and then made herself toast.

The toast was a good call, because the nausea didn't return, and Abby finally started to believe that she was recovering.

THE BELL chimed on the door as Abby walked into Witches in Stitches.

"Abby," Zya said from behind the counter. "It's unusual to see you here on a weekday."

The truth was it was unusual for Abby to be in the store at all. She liked crocheting, but was a crap knitter and hadn't had much time in the past few years to play with yarn at all.

"What can I get for you?" Zya asked, brushing her long dark hair over her shoulder.

"It's more what can you *do* for me," Abby said tentatively.

The other woman's eyebrows rose. "Is something wrong, Abby?"

"No. I…" She shook her head. "I don't think so, but something strange happened yesterday, and I'm still trying to figure it out. I was hoping you might be able to help."

"Did you see a ghost?" Zya asked matter-of-factly as if that was something that happened regularly.

Though Abby supposed it did for Zya. That's why Abby had come to her. The two people in town that were known for seeing and interacting with ghosts were Zya Rossi and Brinn Taylor. Brinn was the cousin of Abby's best friend, and while she might have been the obvious choice to ask for help, Abby just didn't want her friends to know that she was seeing Charlotte. She didn't want to have to see their sympathetic expressions or be reminded of the painful years Abby had suffered after her friend's death. She'd moved on and found happiness. Revisiting that time just wasn't something she wanted to do.

"Yes. My best friend who passed when we were eighteen showed up twice yesterday, but she didn't speak to me. She was just there and then disappeared."

"Has she visited you before?"

Abby started to shake her head, but then stopped. "Only in my dreams. I've never seen her ghostly form before."

Zya's green eyes were full of interest as she studied the other woman. "Interesting. Usually when ghosts show up out of the blue, they are there to deliver a message, need help, or are just keeping an eye on their loved one. There's really no way to know for sure unless you ask."

"So... this is normal?" Abby asked, not exactly sure how she felt about being haunted. On the one hand, she was thrilled to see her friend again. On the other, it was unnerving to think that someone could be watching her at all times. As much as she loved and missed Charlotte, having her friend back in her life as a ghost wasn't something Abby had bargained for.

"For some of us," Zya said with an unconcerned wave. But when she saw Abby's expression, she gave her a sympathetic squeeze of her hand. "It will be okay. Most ghosts are harmless and just want to make a connection to those they left behind. But if you're worried about it, we can do a binding spell to send her away."

That made Abby blink and take a step back. It had never even occurred to her that Charlotte might be some sort of a threat. "No. That's not at all what I want. Charlotte would never hurt me or my family. Not in any form."

Zya nodded. "I'm sure that's true. In my experience, spirits are usually just a freer version of their human selves... with a few exceptions." The shop owner tilted her head to the side. "If you want, we could try to contact her and you can ask why she's appeared now."

Abby's eyes widened. "We could? Now?"

Zya shook her head. "Not here. We'd go to the lagoon on Wanda's property. My power is much stronger when I'm near water."

"Right. Of course." Abby gave her a grateful smile. "Just let me know when you have time. Other than today, I'm busy until next week."

Zya glanced at the clock that was just about to strike noon. "How about today? We can do it on my lunch break."

"Are you sure?" Abby was suddenly nervous. Excited to talk to her friend, but nervous all the same. What did Charlotte have to say?

"I'm sure. Meet me at Incantation Café in thirty minutes. Then we can head over to the lagoon."

"Sounds perfect." Abby paused on the way to the door. "Zya?"

"Yeah?"

"Thank you."

Zya's face softened as she nodded at Abby. "You're welcome."

CHAPTER 5

*A*bby walked up to the counter at Incantation Café and waited patiently for Hanna to notice her. The other woman was busy on the phone, writing down a call-in order. She was dressed in black skinny jeans and a romantic white flowy top that was fashionable and showed off her dark skin. Charlotte's younger sister was the manager at the family's café and was positively glowing.

It made Abby's heart full to know that Hanna was living her best life. They had spent a lot of time together since Abby had move back to Keating Hollow. It helped that Hanna's husband was Clay's assistant at the brewery and was in charge of the hard cider side of the business. Their lives just intersected a lot. Though,

Abby had to admit that since Lynette came along, they hadn't had quite as much quality time together as Abby would've liked.

"Abby!" Hanna exclaimed the moment she hung up the phone. She ran around the counter and engulfed her friend in a tight hug. "I was hoping you'd come in today." She let Abby go and glanced around. "Where's Lynette?"

"She's with Faith's triplets. I have a rare day to myself."

"Seriously? How many times has that happened in the past two years?" she asked with a chuckle.

"I bet I could count the days on one hand," Abby said with an easy smile. Despite her time no longer being her own, she wouldn't change a thing. She loved the life she'd created with Clay.

Hanna returned to her spot behind the counter. "What do you want today? Hot chocolate or something else?"

"Chai tea please. And a coffee cake." Abby reached for her wallet, but Hanna waved her off.

"I've got this today. Go take a seat and I'll join you in a minute." Hanna got busy on Abby's order before Abby could protest.

A few minutes later, Hanna placed a tray with two cups and two pastries on the table and slid into the chair across from her. She jerked her head toward the counter. "Candy's covering me."

Candy was Hanna's cousin who was working at the café while she finished up college.

"Now," Hanna said, rubbing her hands together, "tell me everything. What's going on with you?"

Abby felt her cheeks heat as unease settled over her. Normally she could tell Hanna anything. But something held her back from confiding in Hanna about Charlotte's ghost. Of all people, Hanna should be the one she could talk to, but she just couldn't bring herself to say the words out loud. "Did Rhys tell you about the brew tanks?"

Hanna's smile vanished. "Yes. Oh my gosh, it completely slipped my mind. What is Clay going to do?"

"Use my brews. He and Dad tried them yesterday, and they are both over the moon about them. I guess they think they'll be a decent replacement for the batches they lost yesterday. Or at least will get us through the summer until we can get back into full production."

Hanna raised one eyebrow. "And what do you think about them?"

She shrugged. "I don't know. I had a stomach bug yesterday and never did get to try them. But if Dad and Clay are all in, then I guess they must be okay."

Hanna chuckled and shook her head. "I'm guessing they are much better than just okay. You know how high both of their standards are. No way would they be bottling those batches if they didn't think they'd hold up."

"Yeah. You're right," Abby said, knowing her friend was speaking the truth. "I guess I'm just having a hard time believing I got something good on the first try."

"Beginner's luck?" Hanna asked but then wrinkled her nose. "Nah. You've been around the business long enough, I bet you just picked up on technique by osmosis."

They chit-chatted about the upcoming beer festival, Hanna and Rhys's plans for the Solstice and how the kids were doing. Then they made plans for girls' night the following week.

"Drinks down at the river?" Hanna asked. "We'll get Wanda and the golf carts out."

"I'm in!" Wanda said, seemingly appearing out of nowhere. "Just tell me the day and I'll pencil it in."

By the time they made their plans, their girls' night out had turned into multiple invitations to the women of Keating Hollow and a full-on, four-car golf cart race with a grand prize of cold hard cash and opportunities for side bets.

Abby couldn't stop laughing at their suggestions for

magical sabotage, which was just all part of the golf cart-racing shenanigans.

"I'm thinking exploding hot dogs," Hanna said. "Filled with mayo."

Wanda snorted, making Abby gasp for air as another fit of giggles took over.

"I was going to go with unloading bags of poo-pourrii once we're in the lead," Wanda mused.

"Oh, gag," Abby said, pressing a hand to her stomach. She'd been feeling better, but after the giggle fest and the idea of poo-pourrii, her stomach was back to rebelling. "I think I'm going to call it here. Time for me to get on with my day."

Abby stood and was tugging her crossbody bag over her head when Hanna asked, "What are you doing for the rest of the day? Heading to the spa?"

"Nope." Wanda jumped up and took Abby by the arm. "I'm taking her on a tour of our property to show her all the new landscaping."

"You are?" Abby asked her bestie. "Since when?"

"Since now."

They said their goodbyes, hugged Hanna, and then went out front where Wanda's souped-up purple golf cart was waiting for them.

"Wanda, I'm actually supposed to meet Zya right now. I'm going to have to take a raincheck."

"Nah. We're both meeting Zya. I had stopped by her shop just as you left and she mentioned that you looked a little peaked and you could use a ride out to the lagoon." She waved at the golf cart. "Get in. I'll take you."

"Zya told you we're headed to the lagoon?" Abby asked, unable to keep her irritation out of her tone.

"Well, yeah? It's my property. She usually asks when she's going to take someone out there to perform any kind of spell. Was it a secret?" Wanda didn't look offended, just confused. She had every right to be. Abby didn't keep things from Wanda.

"Yes. No." She climbed into the golf cart and clipped on her seatbelt. "Sorry. I don't know why I'm being so weird about this. It's not a secret. I just haven't wanted to talk about it because... you know, it has to do with Charlotte."

"Charlotte?" Wanda asked, sounding surprised as she eased out of the parking space and headed down Main Street to Zya's store. "What about Charlotte?"

"I saw her twice yesterday," Abby said.

"You mean you saw her ghost?" Wanda gasped out. "Why? I mean, what did she say?"

"Nothing. That's the problem. She just appeared suddenly, and I don't know why." Abby chewed on her bottom lip. "She must be trying to tell me something, right?"

Wanda glanced at Abby, frowning. "But you said she

didn't say anything. Wouldn't she have just told you if she was trying to get a message to you?"

"I don't know. That's the problem I'm having. I asked Zya to help me communicate with her because it's driving me nuts. She's come to me in my dreams before, but never like this. And if you can't tell, I'm sort of freaking out."

"I can tell." The lights that covered Wanda's golf cart suddenly flickered to life, even though Wanda hadn't turned them on.

They both looked up at the purple lights.

Abby turned to Wanda. "That's a sign, right? You didn't accidentally turn those on or anything, did you?"

Wanda glanced down at the switch and shook her head. "Look, Abs. The switch is off."

Abby reached down and flipped the switch. Nothing happened. She tried a few more times, but the lights stayed lit. "It's Charlotte. She's here."

Wanda pulled the golf cart to a stop and glanced around, clearly looking for the ghost of their old friend. "I don't see her, Abby. Maybe it's just a short in the switch."

"Maybe."

They pulled to a stop in front of Witches in Stitches. Zya hurried out, put a sign on the door indicating when she'd be back, and then hopped into the golf cart.

"Abby," Zya said, "I hope it's okay that I told Wanda.

It's her property and since she was in the store, I figured I should tell her we'd be out at the lagoon."

Abby waved a hand, indicating it wasn't a bother. "I was a little surprised, but it's fine. Wanda should know anyway. Charlotte was her friend, too."

Wanda flashed Abby a small smile and took off down the road toward her property.

On any other ride in the golf cart, Abby would have felt carefree. Tooling around town with her best friend on a spring-like day was just about one of her favorite activities. But today, she was just unsettled. Something was off and she wasn't sure it was just because Charlotte had suddenly popped back into her life.

When Wanda steered the golf cart onto the uneven dirt path that led to the lagoon, Abby grabbed the handle on the side of the cart and tried to steady herself. The bumpy ride wasn't sitting right with her still shaky stomach issues.

"Are you okay?" Wanda asked her.

"I'll be fine. I just had a twenty-four-hour stomach thing and am still not quite right, apparently."

Wanda side-eyed her. Then her lips curved up as she asked, "Twenty-four-hour stomach thing? Are you sure you're not pregnant again?"

"What?" Abby shook her head. "No. That's..." She paused, trying to remember when her last cycle had been.

"Oh!" Wanda's eyes widened. "You *are* pregnant!"

Abby pressed a hand to her stomach. "I really don't think so."

"But you don't know?" her friend pressed.

"Well, we weren't trying or anything. Plus, with Lynette I was sick as a dog in the mornings. This morning I was fine. I don't think that's it."

"You should go see Gerry just to make sure," Wanda said and turned right to maneuver through a line of trees.

"Yeah. I guess I should," Abby agreed and then started to wonder if that's why Charlotte was around. Was she the one who'd knocked the beer out of Abby's hand the previous afternoon? A small seed of hope started to blossom in Abby's chest. Another baby? She and Clay had talked about it, but neither had been in a hurry after Lynette was born. But if she was pregnant... Her eyes misted at the thought.

Zya leaned forward from her spot behind Abby and squeezed her shoulder. "How would you feel about that?"

"Ecstatic," she admitted. "And even though our lives are more than a little hectic right now, I know Clay would be, too."

"Then I hope it turns out to be true. If not, then I suppose you'll just have to try harder." She gave Abby an exaggerated wink and then sat back in her seat, chuckling.

Wanda threw her head back and laughed. "Those two? Try harder? I'm not sure their bedsprings could handle it."

"Wanda," Abby said, shaking her head, but her lips were curled into an amused smile.

"Oh, come on, Abs. Don't deny it. With the way that man looks at you, I'm willing to bet you haven't had a decent night's sleep since you moved in."

"We should all be so lucky," Zya said with a sigh.

Wanda raised her eyebrows in question at the woman sitting in the back. "Are you trying to say that you and that hot man of yours aren't in the running for sexiest couple of Keating Hollow?"

Zya gave her a noncommittal shrug and sat back in her seat.

"That's what I thought," Wanda said with a short nod.

"What about you, Wanda?" Abby asked, eyeing her friend. "How are things with Cam?"

Wanda pulled the golf cart to a stop and turned to look at Abby. "Let's just say he's not going to be a candidate for those little blue pills any time soon."

All three women cracked up.

Then the air shifted and Abby suddenly stopped

laughing. She scanned the area, her eyes landing on a figure standing down by the edge of the water.

"There," Abby whispered, pointing. "Do you see her?"

"Charlotte." Wanda said, her tone full of awe. "She looks so... healthy."

"She does," Abby said softly. The last time they'd seen their friend, she'd been thin and fragile after spending her life battling a debilitating disease. This version, the ghostly version, looked radiant and, if possible, happy.

"It's too bad Hanna isn't here," Wanda said.

Abby instantly felt shame. Why had she kept this from her friend's sister? She didn't remember anymore. "I should have asked her to come."

"I don't think so," Zya said. "We still don't know why Charlotte has been seeking you out. It's possible she wouldn't have appeared if her sister was here."

"Why?" Abby asked.

Zya shrugged. "Ghosts only have so much energy, and being near a family member, especially one as close as a sister, could be very draining. It's better that you go talk to her. If Charlotte has a message for her sister, she'll find a way to visit her."

"She's visited Hanna in her dreams occasionally," Abby said. It was a conversation they'd had before. "But never like this. Neither of us have seen a ghost before. I didn't even know that was one of my gifts."

"Magical gifts can change over time," Zya said. "Wanda, have you seen ghosts before?"

"Only here," Wanda said. "When you summon them, sometimes I can see an outline. But never anywhere else."

Abby ignored the conversation and slid out of the golf cart. Tentatively, she made her way down to the water's edge, stopping when she was right next to her friend. "Charlotte?"

The ghost turned to meet Abby's eyes and smiled warmly at her.

Abby was desperate to wrap her friend in a hug but knew how irrational that would be. Instead, she turned to face her and said, "I've missed you."

Charlotte nodded.

"You're here to tell me something, right?" Abby asked.

Her friend nodded again, this time with her expression pinched.

"A warning?"

More nodding.

"About what?"

Charlotte didn't acknowledge that Abby had spoken again. Instead, she stared past Abby, her eyes unfocused as if she was lost in another reality.

"Charlotte?" Abby tried again, moving so that she was right in front of her friend's gaze. "I know you're here to warn me about something, but I don't know what it is. Am I pregnant? Do you want me to be careful? Is that why you knocked the beer out of my hands?"

Charlotte didn't answer. Instead, she mouthed the word *danger* and then faded away.

Abby stared at the spot where her friend had been floating and blinked back tears. The next thing she knew, Wanda was there, hugging her. Abby pressed her face into Wanda's shoulder and sniffed softly. "I miss her so much."

"Me, too, Abs. Me, too."

The pair stood there for a long moment until Abby felt a gentle nudge on her calf. She glanced down and spotted a pure white wolf, sitting patiently beside her, his blue eyes boring into hers. Abby sucked in a sharp breath, startled by the magnificent creature. But his serene presence calmed her in a way she hadn't expected.

"Abby, meet Silver," Zya said. "He's sort of my protector. But it looks like he might be interested in watching over you for a bit."

"What?" Abby glanced from the wolf to Zya. "I can't have a wolf hanging out in my house. I have a teenager as well as a toddler. Not to mention a golden retriever that has more energy than the North Star."

Zya gave her a patient smile. "Silver wouldn't come into your house even if you invited him. But he will watch over your house and family. You likely won't even notice him. Not unless you're looking for him."

"Do I have a choice in the matter?" Abby asked.

"Sure," Zya said, frowning. "But considering you just got a warning from your friend, are you sure this is something you want to turn down?"

Abby's gut churned, and suddenly her nausea was back. She pressed a hand to her stomach and shook her head. "I guess not."

"Trust me," Zya said gently. "There's no harm in having him around. And you don't know when you might need him."

Wanda slipped her hand into Abby's and squeezed. "Come on, Abs. Let's go."

Abby let her friend lead her toward the golf cart, but before they reached the vehicle, Abby's head swam and she stumbled. Blackness creeped in at the edges of her vision and before she knew it, she was sinking to the ground.

"Whoa," Wanda said, grabbing her and holding her up. "You just got really pale. I think it's time we got you to the healer. Something isn't right."

Abby swallowed the bile that had risen in the back

of her throat and just nodded. Her friend was right. It was time for a healer.

The three of them were subdued on their ride back into town. The overhead lights had flickered on and off a few times before they finally winked out. No one said anything.

Abby kept seeing Charlotte mouth the word *danger* over and over again in her mind. What did it mean? Who was in danger? Was it Abby? Her girls? Clay? It made her want to gather all her loved ones in one place and keep an eye on them until... Until when? When Charlotte gave the all clear? Would her friend show back up to let her know the danger had passed, or would Abby just live in abject fear for the rest of her life?

She'd just about worked herself into a minor panic attack when the golf cart came to a sudden stop.

"Dammit!" Wanda muttered as she turned the on-switch back and forth repeatedly.

"is it dead?" Abby asked.

"Completely. We're gonna need a tow."

Weariness washed over Abby as she slumped back into her seat. "Of course we are," she said with a sigh. "What else could go wrong today?"

Zya winced.

"What?" Abby asked without looking back at her.

"I just think that's not something I'd put out into the universe. Not after the warning you got today."

"Son of a... You're right. I take it back," she said to the universe. And then before she could say anything else, there was a sharp stab in her gut that made her fold over herself as she let out a cry of pain.

CHAPTER 6

𝒞 lay Garrison sped through town, his hands clutching the steering wheel of his truck in a death grip. The moment he'd picked up the call from Wanda and learned that Abby had passed out, he'd been in a blind panic. He'd known she'd been feeling off, but not off enough that she'd pass out while sitting in Wanda's golf cart.

Sweat broke on the back of his neck as his worst nightmares flashed through his mind. "No!" He ordered himself to stop thinking the worst. She had to be okay. There was no other option.

He jerked to a stop in a parking space right in front of the healer's office. He had the door open and was already climbing out just seconds after he'd slammed the gear into Park. He took off at a run, rushing into the office and up to the reception desk. "Where's Abby?"

"Mr. Garrison," the young receptionist said, glancing up at him with kindness. "Your wife is still being evaluated by Healer Whipple. If you'll just give us a little time—"

"I'm not waiting. I want to see my wife now," he demanded, cutting her off.

"Clay," a familiar voice said from behind him. "She's okay."

He spun and spotted Wanda standing just across the room. "She's okay? You said she passed out. That's not okay." He started to move toward the door that led to the patient rooms. "Healthy people don't just pass out for no reason."

"Mr. Garrison!" The receptionist jumped up from her chair and ran to stand in front of Clay. "I can't just let you go in there. It's not—"

"It's okay, Bethany," Gerry Whipple said as she walked into the lobby. The gray-haired healer gave Clay a kind smile. "Abby is asking for you."

Clay let out a slow breath. "Okay. Take me to her."

Gerry opened the door and led him down the hall to the last room on the left. "Go on in. I'll be right back."

He paused. "What's wrong with her?"

"I'm still working on a diagnosis, but for now, rest

assured that her vitals are good and there's no indication that she's in any immediate danger."

That didn't exactly put him at ease, but it was something. He nodded. "Okay. Thanks." Then he slipped into the room and silently closed the door behind him.

"Clay," Abby said, her face as pale as the sheet she was lying on.

"Abs." He took two long steps and was by her side, his hand covering hers. "What happened, love?"

"I don't know. Stomach bug? Flu? Food poisoning? All I know is that I was doing okay one minute and the next I was hunched over in pain. And then I woke up here."

"Pain? In your stomach? Like maybe appendicitis or a gall bladder attack?" he asked, his eyes roaming over her as if he had some sort of X-ray vision.

She shook her head. "Gerry checked." Abby's voice was barely audible as she added, "Right after she checked to see if I was pregnant."

"Pregnant?" Clay asked, alarmed. "You might be pregnant, and you had stomach cramps?"

"I'm not pregnant. Gerry scanned me with her magic and she said she doesn't see a second life." There was sadness in his wife's tone, and he realized that she'd gotten her hopes up. He might have too if he'd been thinking she might be with child.

Clay sat down on the exam table next to her and wrapped his arm around her shoulders. "Are you okay?"

She nodded once. "I guess once I let myself believe it was a possibility, I just really wanted it to be true." She glanced up at him, her eyes huge. "You know?"

"Yeah. It's gonna take me a minute to catch up, but I can see that." He swept a lock of hair off her cheek and tucked it behind her ear before leaning down and kissing her tenderly on her temple.

Neither of them said anything while they both let the moment sink in.

Finally Clay said, "Are we ready for another baby?"

"I don't know," Abby said tiredly. "If you'd asked me a few days ago, I'd have said no. Not yet. Lynette is only two and Olive is in her teenage years. Our work lives are busy. Adding another baby seems overwhelming, but when I really stop and think about it, there isn't anything I want more."

"You amaze me. Do you know that?" he asked, holding her close.

"Why?" She was staring up at him with open curiosity as if she really didn't understand that she blew him away on a regular basis.

"You have the biggest heart of anyone I've ever met. Your love is endless, and the day you walked back into Keating Hollow was the day I started really living again. Each milestone we share makes our life fuller, richer, and sweeter. And you handle it all with grace. I'd be crazy not to want another child with you."

"Really?" she breathed as her eyes shone with unshed tears.

"Yes, really. But not until we're sure you're healthy, okay? Risking your health is not an option. Deal?"

"Deal," she said as a lone tear finally rolled down her cheek.

"Knock, knock," Gerry said as she poked her head into the room. "Are you two ready for me?"

"Yes," Abby said, pushing herself up so that she could give the healer her full attention.

Clay stayed where he was, unable and unwilling to let go of his wife.

"Do you have any answers?" Abby asked.

Gerry took a seat and placed a chart on the counter behind her. "Unfortunately, no. I don't have any definitive answers. I can rule out pregnancy, appendicitis, and a gall bladder attack. Any of those would've shown up on my magical scan. That means you likely have some sort of virus."

"What type of virus?" Clay asked. "How worried should we be about this?"

"Let's not worry until there's something to worry about, okay?" Gerry said, still using her kind healer voice.

Clay narrowed his eyes at her. "That's what medical

professionals say when they don't have answers to anything."

The healer nodded, acknowledging his statement. "I can't argue with that. The truth is, we won't know until we run some more tests. The results won't be in until next week. Until then, Abby, I want you to get plenty of fluids and plenty of rest."

"Bed rest?" she asked with a grimace.

"No. That shouldn't be necessary. But if you get light headed again or you start to feel worse, I would like you to get off your feet. The herbs I prescribed should help with your energy. Take them once in the morning and once at night. And if you are trying for a baby, they won't harm anything."

Abby leaned back into Clay, her entire body relaxing. "So that's it. Lots of liquids and the magic herbs until we hear back on Monday?"

"Exactly," Gerry said, getting to her feet. "Now all I need is a blood test, and then Clay can take you home."

Ten minutes later, with a cotton ball taped to her arm, Clay led Abby out into the lobby.

Wanda, who was still in the waiting room, jumped up and came rushing over. "What's the verdict?"

"Still alive." Abby gave her a tired smile.

"Healer Whipple thinks it's just a virus," Clay explained. "Rest and healing herbs are what's on her agenda for the next few days."

Abby let out an impatient huff. "I have to work at the brewery tomorrow."

"No you don't," Clay insisted. "That can wait until early next week. I already told you nothing is more important to me than my family. When you're feeling better, we can worry about starting another batch of beer."

"He's right, Abs. You need to rest." Wanda's gaze swept over her friend and landed at her belly. When she lifted her gaze, a silent communication passed between the two best friends.

Abby shook her head and then looked away.

Clay knew then that the pair had talked about the possibility of a pregnancy, and his heart broke for his wife all over again. She was still too raw from coming to terms with her reality. He hated that she'd had to be reminded that she was, in fact, not pregnant.

"Clay, can you give me a lift?" Wanda asked. "My golf cart is still having issues."

"It just stopped working?" Clay asked as the three of them slipped out of the healer's office.

"Just stopped," she confirmed. "Even the overhead lights had a freak out. Zya called Brody to pick us up, and after he dropped us off here, he took her back to her shop. Cameron is having it towed back to the house. He'll take a look at it later."

"That's decidedly very unlucky," Clay said.

"It is, isn't it?" Wanda said, climbing into the back seat of the truck.

"Let's hope this is the start of a new lucky streak," Abby said.

"I'd drink to that," Wanda said, holding up an imaginary glass.

"Me, too," Clay chimed in. "We're due for a break."

Twenty minutes later, when Clay pulled into the driveway of the home he shared with Abby, the flashing lights from the deputy sheriff's vehicle nearly blinded him in the rearview mirror. His brother-in-law, Drew Baker, got out of the Jeep and hurried over to where Clay stood by the side of his truck.

"Drew? What's happened?" Abby asked, craning her neck out of the truck door.

"I have some bad news," Drew said.

Clay strode over to Abby's door, pulled it open, and then helped his wife out of the seat. They both turned and looked at Drew. Abby, having always been the braver of the two of them, was the one who cleared her throat and said, "We're ready. What is it, Drew?"

He fiddled with the ball cap he wore as he met Abby's worried gaze. "It's your mother. She's been arrested... again."

CHAPTER 7

"*A*rrested?" Abby asked, feeling a ball of unease form in her gut. Her relationship with her mother was complicated. Or more like nonexistent these days. Gabrielle Townsend was an addict who'd left her family when Abby was just eight years old. She'd tried to reconnect with her daughters in the last five years, but with all the abandonment issues the Townsend sisters had, as well as their mother's ongoing addiction issues, those relationships hadn't recovered in the slightest. For the past few years, as far as Abby had known, her mother had been living down in Mendocino county. "She was back here in Keating Hollow?"

"Yes," Drew said. "She was driving through town today, lost control of her vehicle and ran into a street lamp just outside of the inn. When the paramedics got there, it was obvious she was under the influence of something. That's when I was called."

"Was she there to try to see Noel?" Abby asked automatically. Her sister owned the inn, and of the four sisters, she was the least likely to give their mother a shot at redemption.

"Yes," he said with a nod. "Gabrielle kept going on about needing to make amends and if she could just get Noel to forgive her, then everyone else would follow."

"Delusional," Abby said, not bothering to hide her disgust.

"Very," Drew agreed. "Noel is the one who saw the accident and called the paramedics."

"Is she okay?" Abby asked.

"Your mom? She's kind of out of it, but not seriously hurt."

Abby shook her head. "That's good, but I meant Noel. How is she handling this?"

Drew shrugged one shoulder. "You know Noel. It's hard to say. She's angry. But who knows how she'll feel tomorrow?"

"Probably angrier," Abby said with a sad smile. It would take a while for Noel to feel anything else. There was so much resentment tied up with their mother, that anything else would be buried deep in her sister's psyche.

"You're not wrong there," Drew said, blowing out a breath. "I just wanted you guys to hear it from me instead of the town gossip."

"What about Yvette, Faith, and Hope?" Clay asked. "Do they know yet?"

"No. I'm on my way to touch base with them now."

"Want me to come with you?" Clay asked.

The tension in Abby's shoulders eased a little as she glanced up at her husband. How had she gotten so lucky? Clay Garrison would do anything for her and her family. It was something she'd never take for granted.

"It's okay," Drew said. "Thanks, but after the day Abby's had, I think she'd rather you stay here. I can handle it."

"Thanks, man." Clay held his hand out to his brother-in-law and they shook.

Abby stepped up and gave him a hug. "Give Noel my love. Tell her to call if she needs to talk."

"I will." Drew stepped back, gave them a short nod, and climbed back into his cruiser.

"Come on." Clay wrapped his arm around Abby's shoulders and led her into their house. Marina, Clay's mom, was in the kitchen, pulling a fresh pan of focaccia bread out of the oven, while Olive was sitting with Lynette in the middle of the living room, playing with a couple of Lynette's stuffed animals.

Abby sagged into Clay's chest, pausing to just watch them for a moment.

Endora, the dog who usually had more energy than a Tasmanian devil, got up and gingerly walked over to Abby and nudged her hand.

"Hey, girl," Abby said softly to the golden retriever as she scratched her ears. "Thanks for keeping an eye on our girls."

The dog leaned her entire body into Abby's legs, appreciating the affection.

"Abby," Olive said, her young eyes full of concern. "Are you okay? Dad said you passed out."

"I'm fine. Just a virus," she said. "I have orders to rest, so it looks like it's gonna be me and the couch for the weekend."

"There's soup on the stove," Marina said, moving from the kitchen to the living room. She kissed Clay on the cheek and then kissed Abby on the forehead. "Feel better, sweet girl."

Abby smiled gratefully at her. "What would we do without you?"

"You'd manage, but your focaccia intake would suffer." She winked at her. "I've got to get going, but one of you call and let me know how you're doing."

"We will," Abby promised.

She turned to her son. "Take care of this one. I'll talk to you tomorrow." Marina said goodnight to the kids and then waved as she disappeared out the front door.

"How about I just tuck you into bed," Clay said, already tugging her toward the bedroom. "After you're settled, I'll take care of dinner and then get Lynette ready for bed."

His words were like music to her ears, and she surrendered herself to her very capable husband.

Twenty minutes later, Abby was propped up in bed with the TV remote in her hand when Olive walked in with a cup of tea.

"Dad said you might want this." She placed the cup on the bedside table and then stood awkwardly at the side of the bed with her hands in her pockets.

"Thanks, Olive." She reached out, taking the teenager's hand. "And thank you for watching Lynette. Your dad and I appreciate it."

"No worries. I like hanging out with Lynnie. She's fun... when she isn't having a meltdown." Olive gave Abby an eyeroll. "I swear, the time it takes for her to go from laughing to screaming is impressive sometimes."

Abby could only laugh. "You're not wrong about that. The trick to stopping that is correctly anticipating what's going to set her off. Usually she's just tired."

"Or she just wants you," Olive said dismissively.

Abby swallowed the lump that suddenly formed in her throat. It was true. Lots of times, her child just wanted to be comforted by Abby. But these last couple of days, Abby hadn't exactly been present, and she was starting to miss her little girl. Now that she knew she likely had a virus, she wasn't going to get any cuddle time soon.

"Abby?" Olive shifted from side to side, looking uncomfortable.

"Yeah?" She kept her attention on her stepdaughter, wondering what was bothering her.

Footsteps sounded in the hall and a moment later, Clay appeared with a tray in his hands. "Dinner is served." He skirted around Olive and placed the tray on Abby's lap.

"Chicken noodle?" Abby asked, eyeing the bowl and the hunk of focaccia bread he'd included.

"Yep. Mom's chicken noodle is magic. I bet you feel better in no time." He leaned down and kissed the top of her head before cupping her cheek.

Olive let out a groan and mumbled something about PDA before disappearing out of the bedroom.

Abby sighed.

"What was that about?" Clay asked, staring at the spot where his daughter had been a few seconds before.

"I don't know. I think she was about to ask me something. Or maybe confess something? She had that look she gets when there's something on her mind but she isn't sure how to talk about it."

"And I came blundering in, interrupting?" he asked with his eyebrows raised.

"Pretty much." She gave him a soft smile and placed her hand over his that was still cupping her cheek. "But thank you for dinner. You're the best husband in the world."

"You don't really have anyone to compare me to, but I'll take the compliment," he said with a wink.

"I've seen enough to know just how good we have it," she said, smiling at him. Then she sobered. "Can you take some time to talk to Olive? Make sure she's okay?"

"I will, love." He kissed her cheek. "Now eat dinner and get some rest. I've got the rest of this covered."

Abby watched her husband go, and once she was alone, she took a few bites of the soup, but her appetite just wasn't cooperating. After trying a few more times, she set the tray aside and snuggled down into her bed. Moments later, she fell into a deep sleep.

Crash!

Abby bolted upright, adrenaline coursing through her veins. She blinked rapidly, trying to focus in the darkness. "Clay?"

The door opened and Olive walked in, her face white and her eyes wide.

"Olive? What happened?" Abby asked, already climbing out of bed.

"It's Dad," she said in a shaky voice. "A shelf fell and he cut his hand. There's blood everywhere."

Abby threw her robe on and practically ran into the kitchen, finding her husband leaning against the counter with a blood-soaked dish towel wrapped around his left hand. "Clay," she said as she started toward him.

"Stop!" Clay ordered. "The glass." He nodded toward the floor in front of him.

Abby paused to take in the scene. It looked like an entire shelf of drinking glasses had come down and were now shattered on the floor. She turned to her stepdaughter, who was hovering behind her. "Olive, go get the broom and the dust pan from the hall closet."

"Okay." She hurried out of the room.

"Clay, how bad is it?" she asked softly.

When he looked up, his face was pale and there was pain in his expression.

"Never mind. I'll call Gerry." Abby found her phone still in her bag that she'd left by the door and called the healer. A minute later, she ended the call and said, "Come on. Gerry will meet us at the office."

"We have to clean up this glass first," he said through clenched teeth.

Abby hated to take the time to do anything while he was bleeding all over himself, but she couldn't deny he had a point. She didn't want to leave the chore to Olive.

It was too big of a mess. "Right. You go sit in the truck. I'll be right there."

Clay carefully made his way through the mess while Abby found a paper garbage bag and started to carefully pick up the larger glass pieces.

"Abby?" Olive said from behind her. "Want me to sweep?"

"No, sweetheart. I've got it. If you can just keep an eye on Lynette for a while, that would be a lifesaver."

"Sure." Olive paused before retreating down the hallway. "Is Dad going to be okay?" Her tone held so much worry that it made Abby stop what she was doing and walk over to the teenager.

Abby gave her a hug and whispered, "He'll be fine. I bet by the time Gerry is done with him, he'll have a bionic hand."

Olive hugged her tighter, and her voice was muffled when she said, "He doesn't need a bionic hand. He just needs to be okay."

Oof. Obviously, it wasn't the time for jokes. "He will be. I promise."

Olive released her and immediately started sweeping up the glass. "I've got this. Just take Dad to the healer."

"Not until we have this cleaned up." Abby would have just done it herself, but Olive seemed determined. So together, they cleared the kitchen of the glass and then Abby kissed Olive on the top of the head and hurried out to find her husband slumped against the passenger window of the truck.

"Clay?" she said as she pressed the button to start the truck.

He blinked his eyes open. "Yeah?"

"Just checking in." She noted that the towel was saturated with blood, and laid into the accelerator as they sped down the road.

CHAPTER 8

*C*lay tossed the two pain relievers in his mouth and tried to ignore the ache in his hand. It had been thirty-six hours since he'd earned himself forty-two stitches and a tetanus shot. *Forty-two stitches.*

That was more than inconvenient when he had to unload the truck and set up for a beer festival. He gritted his teeth and reached into the bed of his truck to load another case of beer onto the dolly.

"Drop it," a familiar masculine voice ordered.

Clay turned to find his assistant, Rhys Silver, standing behind him, and Clay frowned in confusion. "Rhys? What are you doing here? I thought you were overseeing the brewery today."

"Lincoln sent me." He gently nudged Clay out of the

way and grabbed the case. "You're in no condition to be setting up a booth."

"That's what Abby told him," Olive said from the other side of the truck. She had her arms folded over her chest and was staring at her father with undisguised judgment.

"I had to show up," Clay said, defending himself. "We entered the stout into the competition, plus we need to get people on board with our changes. Otherwise—"

"Otherwise, we'd lose money this summer," Rhys finished for him. "We're all aware, brother. But we also can't have you tearing those stitches out. So we're making it work. Go on and do your networking. I'll get the tent set up."

"I'll help," Olive said and started pulling boxes from the truck to load onto the dolly.

Clay's daughter had gotten up early and insisted on accompanying him to the festival. She'd said someone needed to keep an eye on him. He'd actually wanted her to stay home with Abby, as she still wasn't feeling quite right. She wasn't passing out anymore, but she was still nauseated and had developed a slight headache. But Abby had told her to go, insisting that Wanda was planning to come spend time with Lynette and would keep an eye on her. Clay hadn't been crazy about leaving her, but he really didn't have a choice. It made him feel a little better to know that Wanda would be around. She'd be sure to keep an eye on his wife and daughter.

"Dad?" Olive called.

"Yeah, sweetheart?" He turned to find her brushing her dark hair out of her eyes. "Can I have the truck keys?"

"Sure." He fished his keyring out of his pocket and handed it to her. "Did you forget something in the cab?"

She shook her head. "No. I just wanted the music on while we unload."

Of course she did. Olive was in her classic rock appreciation stage. Clay was rather enjoying that they had something to talk about. "My Fleetwood Mac CD is in the glove compartment."

"It is?" Her eyes lit up. "Perfect."

"Fleetwood Mac?" Rhys asked, a pleasantly surprised look on his face.

"Of course," Olive said. "They're all the rage on TikTok. Keep up, Uncle Rhys."

Clay chuckled. "Yeah, keep up, Uncle Rhys. Didn't you see that video of the guy on the skateboard? It went viral, and the next thing you know, 'Rumors' is topping the charts again."

"I feel so old right now," Rhys muttered to himself. "I don't even know what TikTok is."

Olive gasped as if she were scandalized and quickly

pulled out her phone to introduce him to the wildly popular social media app. Clay just walked away chuckling.

Clay spent the next few hours talking to various vendors, hyping up their new line of beers, and inviting them to his booth. By the time he returned to the booth, Rhys had already poured dozens of samples and had taken an impressive number of orders for both current and new clients while Olive handed out small bottles of water. "Wow," he said, looking over the order log. "This is impressive."

"I'd say that's the work of Abby's beer," Rhys said. "You should have seen them, Clay. The looks on their faces when they tried the French Toast Porter would have made you think they'd won the lottery. Abby really hit on something special."

"She did," he agreed.

Rhys pushed himself up out of his chair and started hobbling over to where Clay was standing.

"Dude. What happened?" Clay asked, putting the tablet down on the table.

"I just twisted my ankle. It's not that big a deal," he said even as he winced from the pressure on this foot.

"You can barely walk. Sit down," he ordered. "I'll get you some ice." He glanced at Olive, who was hovering nearby, her face grim. "Keep an eye on him until I get back. Don't let him walk on that ankle."

She nodded and went to stand right next to Rhys, placing her small hand on his shoulder.

Rhys glanced up at her in mock exasperation. "You don't need to hold me down. I can take orders from the boss."

"Doubtful. You didn't listen to me when I told you not to walk on it," she said, giving him her signature teenage eyeroll.

Clay's lips twitched as he watched the interaction, but then he put his head down and headed for the ice vendor.

The day went by quickly. By the time five rolled around, Abby's stout had won a blue ribbon, they were flush with orders, and Hanna and her cousin Candy had arrived to collect Rhys and his vehicle. After loading up, Clay thanked Hanna and Candy for their help. He ordered Rhys to get to the healer and then they waved as Hanna and Rhys left in her car while Candy drove Rhys's back to Keating Hollow.

"Ready, kid?" Clay asked his daughter.

She gave him a tired but happy smile. "Sure. Can we stop for some ice cream on the way home?"

He laughed. "Okay. But what about dinner?"

"Remember those hot dogs? I'm good."

He nodded. They had eaten a late lunch. "You're on. I'm just going to check the booth area one more time to make sure we have everything."

As Olive climbed into the truck, Clay hurried back to their assigned area. It had come with a tent and a table. Once he was satisfied they hadn't left anything behind, he stopped at the restroom and then headed toward the truck. Along the way, he spotted a couple of squirrels that were chasing each other around a tree. One stopped suddenly and picked up something off the ground. The sunlight hit the red jewel as the squirrel tried to bite it. When it was apparent the object wasn't food, the squirrel quickly dropped it just a few feet from Clay.

He paused and then frowned when he recognized the crystal as the one Olive had given him just days before. It was on a small chain with a distinctive brass clasp that had a pentagram engraved on the face. He quickly snatched it up and shoved it into his pocket. It must have somehow gotten disconnected from his keychain.

Whistling softly to himself and pleased with the day, he made it back to the truck and said, "Ready for that ice cream?"

"Ready," Olive agreed and pressed play on the CD player. Fleetwood Mac streamed from the speakers as his daughter started to sing along with Stevie Nicks.

CHAPTER 9

"It's gorgeous out here today," Wanda said, tilting her head back to let the sun shine down on her face.

"It really is," Abby agreed. Not long after Clay and Olive had left, she'd finally started to feel better. After some toast and a pain reliever, her nausea and headache had disappeared, much to her relief. She prayed it was the end of the virus that plagued her.

It was late afternoon and they were sitting out on the back patio, relaxing with iced tea while Lynette played on a blanket at Abby's feet.

"I see Silver is still keeping an eye on you," Wanda said, eyeing the pure white wolf who was pacing at the edge of the tree line. "Has anything unusual happened since Charlotte's warning?"

"No. Nothing. But this is the first time he's been pacing. Normally he just sits there, watching." Abby eyed the wolf and tried to ignore the feeling that something was off. She was finally feeling better. And Clay and Olive were at the festival with Rhys. If something was wrong, one of them would call. Right?

But why was the wolf pacing? Suddenly the wolf stopped and bolted back into the woods.

"That was strange," Wanda said, frowning in the direction where the wolf had disappeared.

"You can say that again." Abby reached down and picked Lynette up, holding the little girl close.

The toddler pressed her hand to her lips, smacking it with a kiss and then pressing her hand to her mother's face as she laughed.

Abby grinned at her daughter. "You're such a flirt." She gave her child a loud smacking kiss on the cheek and pushed all her worries aside. It was a gorgeous day and she was going to enjoy every moment of it, despite Charlotte's warning and the run of bad luck they'd had recently. Life was too short to focus on the negative.

AFTER CLAY and Olive had filled their bellies with ice cream, Clay drove them through town and turned onto the two-lane highway that led back into Keating Hollow.

Olive reached over to turn the music down and then turned to her father. "Dad?"

"Yeah, sweetie?" He kept his eyes on the road. The sun was setting and it wasn't unusual for wildlife to make an appearance in the fading twilight.

"What do you do if you like someone?"

Clay glanced over at his daughter to find her staring at her hands and wished he wasn't driving on a winding two-way road. His heart was in his throat as he tried to figure out how to navigate this conversation. "When you say you like someone, do you mean you have a crush?"

"No one says crush, Dad," she said, sounding exasperated.

"Sorry," he said with a soft chuckle. "You'll have to excuse my old-man status. I've already resigned myself to the fact that I'm very much *not* cool. But I still might have some decent advice."

"Well, duh. That's why I asked you."

Clay bit back a grin and cleared his throat. "So, you like someone romantically and you're not sure what, if anything, you should do about it?"

"Yeah." Her voice was very quiet as she stared out the window.

"Okay, well, I suppose it depends on the relationship

you have with them now. Are you friends, or is this person an acquaintance?"

"He's newish in town and in two of my classes. I don't know if I'd say we're friends, but we are paired up to work on a project together."

"Hmm. Interesting," Clay said, trying to sound thoughtful even though he was freaking out inside. It wasn't that he hadn't expected her to start to show an interest in dating, but she was just fourteen. She was his baby. He wasn't ready.

"Dad?" she asked when he didn't continue. "Are you in there? What did you do when you knew you liked Abby?"

He swallowed hard. He couldn't remember a time when he wasn't in love with Abigail Townsend. "I, uh, I guess I just asked her out. From there, everything just fell into place."

"That's not helpful." She crossed her arms over her chest.

This time he couldn't stifle his smile. "Listen, kid. Relationships at any age are confusing. I guess the best thing I can say is just be honest. If you like this guy and want to spend time with him outside of school, then invite him to the café or on a hike or something you think both of you will enjoy. If he's interested, he'll agree. If not, then you're better off knowing sooner rather than later, right?"

"Your advice is to just ask him out?" Her voice rose a couple octaves.

"Yep. That's the advice. I know it's not easy. No one wants to put themselves out there, but if you don't ask, you won't ever know, right?"

"Ugh."

He reached over to grab her hand and squeezed it lightly before putting his back on the wheel. "What's the worst that could happen?"

"Dad! Look out!" Olive cried.

A family of three deer had jumped into the road. Clay slammed on the brakes and swerved, just barely missing the large buck. The truck fishtailed and then skidded off the road, crashing right through the barrier as the truck went over the embankment and slammed into a large redwood tree.

The airbags went off, and the world seemed eerily silent for a moment as Clay tried to collect his bearings. Suddenly his adrenaline kicked in and he turned to his daughter. "Olive!"

"Ouch," she said, her eyes wide as she stared at him.

He quickly unbuckled himself and ran around the truck and yanked the passenger door open. "Are you hurt?" he asked as he pushed the deflating airbag away and scanned his daughter for injuries.

"I... I don't think so," she said in a shaky voice.

Clay quickly pulled his phone out of his pocket and dialed Drew's number.

"Where did that come from!" Olive yelled, panic in her voice.

As the phone rang, Clay scanned the area, looking for predators or anything else that was dangerous. In the distance, he spotted a familiar pure white wolf that had been watching over their house the past few days. The wolf was pacing, clearly agitated, but he didn't make a move to come closer.

"Silver," he said. "What's he doing out here?"

"Not him," Olive said, her voice cracking. "That!" She pointed to his feet. "That crystal! I thought I got rid of it!"

He glanced down and spotted the red crystal that he'd picked up earlier and shoved into his pocket. It must have fallen out when he'd retrieved his phone. "I found it on the ground just before we left the festival and picked it up. What do you mean you got rid of it? Why?"

"It's cursed!" She jumped out of the truck and reached for it, but Clay grabbed her, stopping her.

"Olive, why do you think it's cursed?" he asked.

"Because. Ever since Abby's mother gave it to me, crazy things keep happening to us. I thought if I got rid of it, they'd stop. But here it is again and we just..." Her lips trembled and tears filled her eyes as she waved at the crumpled truck. "I didn't know, Dad. She told me it was a crystal of protection. Only it's brought us nothing but bad luck!"

"Drew Baker here," Drew said when he answered his phone.

"Drew, it's Clay. Olive and I have had an accident. We'll need a lift and a tow truck. And someone who can handle cursed objects."

CHAPTER 10

*a*bby stared at the red crystal through the protective glass, pure rage coursing through her body. "I want to touch it," she said.

"What? No, Abby. It's cursed," Clay said. "What we need is for someone to destroy it."

"Not until I confirm that my mother cursed it," she insisted. She'd left Lynette with Wanda and met Olive and Clay at the sheriff's department so that Olive could give a statement on how she came into possession of the crystal.

It turned out that Gabrielle had shown up at the music store one day when Olive was there for her piano lessons. She'd acted like it was an accident and was kind to Olive, telling her that she was proud that her granddaughter was learning the piano. She'd talked about learning as a little girl, and then when Olive was leaving, she'd pressed the crystal into her hand and said it was for keeping loved ones safe.

"She told me it worked best when given as a gift to someone you love," Olive said. "I thought that was kind of cool, and when I got home, I gave it to my dad."

"You never told your dad where you got it?" Drew asked.

Olive looked nervous as she glanced around the room, but she shook her head. "I knew that Abby didn't really talk to her mom, but I didn't know all the details. Gabby seemed nice and I don't know, I just felt weird about it, so I didn't say anything about where it came from."

"And when did you start to think that the crystal was cursed?"

"Last night." She chewed on her bottom lip. "Dad and Abby were talking about all the awful things that had been happening lately, and Abby made a joke about someone cursing them. It was then I remembered what her mother had said about the crystal and protection. But when I really thought about it, all the stuff that happened started just after I gave it to my dad. The tank problem at the brewery, Abby getting sick, the golf cart dying, and my dad cutting himself. Then this morning, I'd handed Rhys Dad's keys to lock up the truck and then he sprained his ankle. I figured it had to be the crystal. So I got rid of it." Her voice started to rise to a hysterical level. "But then it seemed to find Dad, and the next thing you know, we're off in a ditch and the truck is wrecked! Everything is my fault!"

Clay wrapped his arms around his daughter and pulled her in for a hug. "It's not your fault, honey. If it's true the crystal is cursed, this is on Gabrielle. Not you. You did nothing wrong. Understand?"

Olive sniffed as the tears ran down her cheeks.

Abby got up and wrapped her arms around her husband and stepdaughter, ignoring the exhaustion that swept over her. "Your dad is right, Olive. You didn't do anything wrong. If anything, you're the hero here for figuring out the problem."

Olive shook in their arms.

Abby met Clay's worried gaze and in that moment, she vowed that her mother would never hurt someone she loved again. If Olive's suspicion was true and the crystal was cursed, there was no excusing what she'd done. Why had she done it? She'd targeted a teenager, for the goddess's sake. None of it made sense. "I have to see that crystal."

"Abs," Clay said. "I don't want you anywhere near it."

"I know," she said softly. "But you and I both know there's a signature left on magical items. If I look for it, I might be able to tell for sure if my mother did this or if she didn't know it was cursed. Either way, she never should have engaged with Olive, but I need to know if she did this on purpose."

A whole range of feelings flashed in Clay's eyes. There was everything from apprehension to pure rage. Abby could relate. Finally he gave her a short nod. "Yeah. Do it."

"No!" Olive said, squirming to get out of their embrace. "I don't want anything else to happen to you guys."

Abby let her stepdaughter go and very gently said, "I'm going to be fine. We'll all be right here in the sheriff's office. It'll only take me a few minutes."

Olive's face was blotchy and the worry in her expression almost made Abby relent, but this was too important.

"I'm sorry. I know this is stressful, but it's just something I have to do." Abby turned to Drew. "Can you take me into the other room?"

"Sure, Abs." Her brother-in-law led her into the evidence room and stood by the door.

"Is it a problem if I touch it?" she asked him. "It's not like my fingerprints aren't already all over it. I've had Clay's keys a few days this past week."

"It's fine. We already dusted it for prints and expect to get multiple results," he said.

She nodded and then sat down at the desk where the offending object was lying by itself on a velvet cloth. Now that she had the suspicion that the crystal was infused with magic, she could feel the faint vibration coming from it. It was barely there, but when one was looking for it, it was hard to miss.

An ominous tingle skated over her skin, and she wondered if that was just nerves or if it was from the crystal. Steeling herself, Abby reached out and clasped her palm around the crystal. Immediately her stomach rolled and her vision turned dark at the edges.

Abby sucked in a sharp breath, willing herself not to pass out. "Focus, Abby," she whispered to herself. Pushing past the nausea that had returned, she searched for a tiny hint of a magical signature.

There was nothing but pain. Her gut started to ache and her eyes watered. Her head swam, and all she wanted to do was let go. But she couldn't. She had to know.

"Show me," she ordered the universe. "Show me who did this."

A faint hint of lavender scented the air, and Abby instantly let go of the crystal. Tears streamed down her face as she pressed her hand to her abdomen. "Drew, get me out of here."

Her brother-in-law moved quickly, wrapping his arm around her shoulders and guiding her out of the small room. As soon as the door closed behind them,

Abby's stomachache vanished and the nausea began to fade.

But the soul-crushing ache of betrayal lingered as she slowly sat down beside her husband.

"It was her. My mother did this." She turned to Olive, her heart aching. "I'm so sorry, sweetie."

Olive reached out and squeezed her hand. "It's not your fault."

"No. But it's not yours either. And I promise you, I'll make sure she never comes near you again." There was a conviction in Abby's voice that even she didn't recognize. Her mama-bear instincts had roared to life, and all she could think was that it was a damned good thing that her mother was already behind bars. Because if she wasn't, Abby would've probably found herself in handcuffs after committing a felony.

"We have everything we need," Drew said gently. "Why don't you guys head to the healer and make sure everyone is all right. I'll give you a call tomorrow after we get a statement from your mother."

Abby desperately wanted to be there when Drew questioned Gabby. But she knew he'd never allow it. She could come back and confront her another time. It wasn't like she was going anywhere anytime soon.

"Come on, Abs," Clay said, tugging her to her feet. "Gerry Whipple is waiting for us."

"Right." Abby stood, took Olive's hand in hers, and

let Clay lead them out into the night air. Without a word, she took her keys out of her pocket, climbed into her SUV, and carefully drove them to the healer. Once Gerry checked them out and prescribed some calming herbs for Olive, she told them they were good to go and to call if any mysterious pains or bruises showed up.

"We will," Clay assured her and then thanked her for all her help the past week.

When they got home, the white wolf was waiting for them near the front porch. As soon as he saw them, he trotted off to the edge of the trees and sat down, keeping a vigilant eye on their family.

Abby eyed the wolf, wary that he was still there. Zya had sent him to watch over them after Charlotte's warning of danger. But if he was still there, did that mean they still weren't out of the woods? A headache formed at her temple, but she didn't think it had anything to do with her mother's crystal. This time, she was certain it was just sheer exhaustion.

"He was there today," Clay said. "When we crashed. He was there, keeping an eye on us until Drew showed up."

"He was?" Abby asked, astonished. "All the way out on the highway?"

He nodded. "I don't know how he knew where to find us, but he was there. It was..." He shrugged. "I don't know, reassuring maybe?"

"He's the protector," Abby said, making a note to herself to thank Zya. "He'd have gotten help if you needed it."

"I think so, too," Olive said.

Abby and Clay watched as Olive slowly made her way to the wolf. He tentatively met her halfway. Once they were a mere foot apart, Olive held her hand out to him. The wolf nudged her hand once and then retreated back to the tree line to keep watch over the family.

"Let's go in," Abby said quietly. "I want to see my daughter, and I'm sure Wanda's ready to go home."

Wanda was curled up on the couch with Lynette, reading a book. The moment Abby walked inside, the little girl came running, and it was everything Abby needed. She'd mouthed *thank you* to Wanda and waved as her friend checked on Clay and Olive. When Wanda was satisfied they were okay, she said she'd call the next day and quietly slipped outside as Abby started another book for Lynette.

Everyone was home and safe, and that was all that matter to Abby. She'd deal with the rest in the morning.

CHAPTER 11

"I'm just not going to rest until that crystal is destroyed," Abby said. She was standing in her kitchen on Saturday morning, nursing a cup of coffee. Her nerves were still on edge, despite the fact that the crystal was no longer in their possession. "How do we know it doesn't have lingering effects?"

"What did Drew say when you spoke to him about it?" Clay asked. He was busy making waffles for brunch. They'd had a quiet evening after they got home, and everyone was still subdued. He thought a big family brunch might help everyone settle after the excitement from the day before. "Do they need it for evidence?"

Abby shook her head. "No. Gabby confessed to everything last night. It looks like she's going to take a plea deal."

"Okay, then we just need to find someone who can neutralize it. How do we do that?"

"I need to do it," Abby said.

Clay suddenly stopped stirring the waffle batter and jerked his head up to look at her. "You? I don't want you near that thing again."

"I know you don't, but the fact is, I'm a very competent earth witch, Clay. And I know how to neutralize these kinds of spells. I used to help my roommate, Lily, do it all the time when I lived in New Orleans. Unless I fly her out here, I think I'm the only one around here with the knowledge to do it."

He blinked at her. "You used to neutralize cursed items when you lived in New Orleans?"

"Yes. There are a lot of them down there, and it was a good side gig for us. She worked for a witch who specialized in spelled objects and learned all about neutralizing curses using herbs. So she opened up a side business, helping out people who had weird cursed objects, and I helped her. Most of them were relatively harmless, but a few were pretty dangerous. I know what I'm doing."

"I'm sure you do, but..." He shook his head. "I don't like it, Abs."

"I know, but this is something I need to do."

They stared at each other for a long moment.

Finally, Clay let out a sigh and nodded. "Do what you need to do."

Abby walked over to him and wrapped her arms around his waist. "I love you."

"I love you, too. That's why I hate this. But I understand the need for closure. Just be careful, okay?"

"I will." She held onto him, pressing her ear to his heart so she could let his heartbeat settle her. When she finally let him go, she gave him a gentle kiss and then grabbed her car keys and headed to Noel's house.

Her sister answered the door, still wearing her pajama pants and a T-shirt. "Abby, are you all right?"

"Not yet, but I will be. Are you?"

"I'm pissed off, but I imagine that will pass eventually." She stepped outside onto her front porch and closed the door behind her before taking a seat on the porch swing.

Abby followed, sitting next to her.

"I'm glad you stopped by," Noel said. "Drew and I were talking about it, and I think we should file a restraining order against Gabrielle. All of us. You, me, Faith, Yvette, and Hope. Drew said we can include our families. No judge would say no to this after what she did."

Abby nodded. "I'm in. How soon can we get it done?"

"Just as soon as we get everyone's signature." Noel

sat back and closed her eyes. "You know, for a while there I really thought she was going to stay away."

"I didn't," Abby said.

Noel opened her eyes and stared at her sister. "No? Has she been contacting you?"

"Not recently." Abby frowned. "But the last time I saw her, she told me she was going to stay clean and wanted a relationship with us. She said she'd prove it. And she's tried to get close to Hope. I just never got the impression that she was going to give up on trying to get us to forgive her."

Noel snorted. "Delusional."

Abby gave her sister a gentle smile. "You know, if it weren't for the fact that she's an addict and keeps doing terrible things, there might have been room to try to rebuild something. I mean, leaving us the way she did was terrible. But if she'd ever gotten sober long enough to do something with her life other than make us miserable, I'd have given her a chance."

"You're a better person than me, Abs." Noel's jaw tightened, and her face was full of undisguised disgust.

Abby knew all that aggression was aimed at their mother. Who could blame Noel for feeling that way? Abby did too most days, but today she was just tired of it all. "I'm on board for the restraining order. I know Mom is going to be serving time, but still, the sooner the better as far as I'm concerned. I don't want any possibility of her writing to any of our kids."

"Holy hell," Noel said, pressing her palm to her forehead. "That never even occurred to me. I'll tell Drew to get the paperwork ready so we can all sign it."

"Speaking of Drew, is he here?"

Her sister dropped her hand. "Yeah. Why?"

"I need to ask him something about that crystal."

Noel nodded and rose from the swing. "I'll be right back."

When the door opened again, Drew joined Abby on the swing. He was wearing jeans and a T-shirt and was carrying a mug of coffee. "How are Clay and Olive today?" he asked.

"They're doing all right," she said. "Olive had a bruise on her arm, and Clay said he felt like he'd been run over by a bus, but considering the impact they had, we're just glad it wasn't worse."

"That's good." He took a sip of his coffee. "Noel said you had questions about the crystal."

"Yes." She turned to him and held his gaze. "What would happen if the crystal was neutralized? Would that have any impact on my mother's case?"

His brow furrowed as he thought it over. "Probably not. She already confessed and a plea deal is being worked out. The only reason we'd need it would be if we went to trial, and even then, we wouldn't allow a cursed item in court. Why? Are you wanting to get someone in to neutralize the curse?"

"I want to do it," she said. "Before you say anything, I have experience in this area. I can do it without hurting myself or anyone else."

"I don't think that's a good idea, Abby. That thing has already done a lot of damage to your family. I can't imagine Clay is on board with this."

"He's not happy about it, but he knows I'm here. Listen, I just need to deactivate it. I need to know it isn't going to end up in the wrong hands or come back to haunt us."

"You mean it will be cathartic for you," Drew said, eyeing her.

"Yes." She crossed her arms over her chest and waited.

"Let her do it, Drew," Noel said from the doorway.

Startled, Abby jerked her attention to her sister. "I didn't even know you were there."

"I'm stealthy like that," she said with a wink. Then Noel turned her attention to her husband. "I'd feel better knowing the curse is gone, too."

Drew pressed his lips together into a thin line and then nodded reluctantly. "Fine. You can neutralize it, but I'm going to need it back for the evidence record."

Abby stood, smiling triumphantly. "Great. Let's go."

"Now?" Drew asked, grimacing. "I haven't even finished my coffee."

"I'll put it in a to-go mug for you, babe," Noel said, grabbing the cup and disappearing back into the house.

Drew stared after her with his mouth hanging open.

Abby chuckled.

He shook his head. "There never is any winning when the Townsend sisters team up, is there?"

"Nope." Abby grinned, feeling better than she had in days.

Drew stood. "Let's go."

Abby waved at her sister and followed Drew off the porch.

"Are you sure you're up to this?" Lincoln Townsend asked Abby. They were standing in her studio behind her father's house. Drew and Clair were waiting outside, both of them doing their best to keep their concerns to themselves.

"I'm sure." She glanced out the window and spotted Silver. The pure white wolf was pacing back and forth just as he had been at her house the past few days.

"Abby—" Lincoln started.

"Dad, seriously. I've got this." She opened the brown paper bag that held the crystal and peeked in, making sure it was still there. The seemingly benign stone was lying there making her wonder how it had caused so much strife over the past week.

Cursed. The word ran through her mind, making her shudder. It was still unbelievable that her mother had actually cursed her family. She still didn't know why, but before the day was over, she was determined to find out. But first she had to neutralize the stone.

Her dad put his hands up and backed away. "Okay. I'll be here in case anything goes awry."

Abby gave him a grateful smile and then turned her attention to the herbs she'd laid out. After pouring a package of stinging nettle into her mortar, she used the pestle to crush it while she sent a steady stream of magic from her fingers into the bowl. Chanting under her breath, she repeated, "From the sun and stars and moon, cleanse the crystal until it's pure and washed anew." Only when the herb was crushed into powder did she add an infusion of mugwort water. The combination was a powerful curse-cleansing agent, but only if her magic was strong enough. Taking a deep breath, Abby picked up the paper bag and carefully turned it over so that the crystal tumbled out and into the mortar.

Only instead of the crystal slipping into the potion she'd just made, it hovered above the concoction, suspended in air.

It was resisting. *Dammit!*

Abby grabbed a fresh wooden spoon, using it as a conductor of her magic, and pointed it right at the crystal. Her magic poured into it, the crystal sucking it up as if it were a shriveled cactus in the middle of the desert. Her head began to ache as sweat formed on the back of her neck.

Her intention was to zap the curse out of the stone, but now she wasn't sure she could make that happen.

Instead, it was time to obliterate it.

Abby grabbed a second wooden spoon, and with both pointing at the stone, she cried, *"Perdere!"*

Her magic turned pure white as the scent of smoke filled her senses. And just as she was starting to believe that her magic wasn't strong enough, the crystal cracked right down the middle and fell unceremoniously into her potion. The liquid sizzled and then turned a putrid shade of green.

Abby dropped the spoons and stumbled backward, her legs shaking.

"I've got you," her dad said, steadying her with both hands.

"Thanks," she said, still trying to catch her breath.

"I think it's fair to say that everything is going to be just fine now, Abigail," Lincoln said.

"You think so?" she asked, glancing back at him. "Just because it broke doesn't mean the spell is gone."

"True," he said thoughtfully. "But as soon as it dropped into your potion, your wolf protector stopped pacing. Look."

Abby glanced out the window and spotted Silver staring at her. When their eyes met, the wolf held her gaze for just a moment before he turned and sauntered back into the woods. It was then she knew her dad was right. The curse was gone.

CHAPTER 12

"*A*re you ready for this?" Lincoln Townsend asked Noel and Abby.

Abby pushed her sleeves up as she stared at the door to the sheriff's office. "No." Abby turned to her sister. "Are you?"

"Are you kidding? I've been waiting years to tell off our mother. I think I'm going to enjoy this far too much."

"That's one way of looking at it," Lincoln said under his breath.

Noel shrugged one shoulder and the gleam in her eyes made Abby laugh. It was a strange sensation. One shouldn't be joking when they were headed in to inform their own mother about a restraining order. But the past week had been so trying that she was just relieved it was almost over. The curse had been lifted. Her mother was going to be serving a minimum of five years. And the brewery had enough orders to get them through the foreseeable future.

"Okay. I'll follow your lead," Abby said, waving for her sister to go ahead of her.

"My pleasure." Noel strode through the door and held it open for her sister and their father. When they'd told their dad about the restraining order and that they were going down to talk to their mother, he'd insisted on coming along. It appeared he had some things he needed to say, too. Their sisters had declined, stating that they had nothing to say to Gabrielle.

Once they were inside, Drew came out of his office immediately to meet them and said, "She's already waiting for you in one of the conference rooms."

"Good. I don't have all afternoon to do this," Noel said. "I have to get the kids in an hour."

"I know," Drew said patiently as he led them back to where one of the other officers was guarding a door. Drew nodded to him and then let Abby, Noel and Lincoln in. "Just knock on the door when you're ready to go."

"Got it," Noel said in her no-nonsense tone.

"Noel? Abby? Lincoln?" Gabrielle said, her face full of hope. "You all came to see me?"

"Just tell us why, Mom," Noel said, standing with her

arms crossed over her chest, glaring down at their mother as Lincoln and Abby sat in chairs across from Gabrielle.

"Why what? Do you mean why I left all those years ago?" she asked, looking confused.

"No," Noel scoffed. "Why did you give Olive a cursed crystal? Do you realize you could've killed her or Abby or Clay? Just what exactly was your end goal?"

"Yes, Gabrielle. Tell us why you endangered my daughter," Lincoln added, his voice low and full of disgust.

Abby stared at her mother, not sure she even wanted to hear the answer. Did it matter? Her mother was a real piece of work and Abby just didn't want anything to do with her.

"She's my daughter, too, Lin," Gabrielle said, her eyes narrowed at him.

"Not anymore," Abby shot back. "Not after this."

Gabrielle swallowed hard, her eyes pleading with Abby as she said, "I just... I miss you girls so much."

"So cursing my family was the answer?" Abby asked in a cold tone, void of feeling.

"That's not..." Gabrielle shook her head. "I guess I thought if some minor things happened, you'd want your mother. That maybe you'd call if things got overwhelming. I could be there to help and things could go back to the way they used to be."

"What in the fresh hell?" Noel muttered.

Abby sat across from her mother, shocked into silence.

"Used to be?" Lin asked incredulously. "You mean before you abandoned them and the rest of us? And then gave Hope up for adoption? You mean like it used to be *then*?" At one point when Gabrielle had shown back up, Lincoln had been civil with her. And even though he hadn't ever understood her choices and struggles, he'd tried to be understanding that people made mistakes and might need a second chance. But it was clear he was well past that now. He was livid with her, and there was no going back.

"I know it wasn't well thought out," Gabrielle tried to explain. "I wasn't really trying to hurt anyone. I just wanted to talk to Abby. I thought—"

"I know what you thought!" Abby shouted at her. "In that addled brain of yours, you wanted me to come running for Mommy. Well, guess what? You're not my mother. The only person I consider my mom is Clair. She's the one who has been there for me and the rest of us over the last twenty years. Not you. You have no idea what love is. Or what it means to be family. You're nothing. And as of today, we're all filing restraining orders against you."

Gabrielle slumped back into her chair and closed

her eyes. "What does it matter? I'll be locked up. It's not like I can show up on your front porch."

"And thank the gods for that!" Abby cried.

"It matters," Noel said, stepping in. "Because it never expires and it means you can't come near or contact any of us. Not me, Abby, Yvette, Faith, Hope, or any of our spouses or children. If you do, your sentence will be extended. Understand?"

Her mouth dropped open. "But the things I did were because of my addiction. You're not really going to cut me off because of my illness, are you? Lincoln, tell them," she pleaded with him.

"No, Gabrielle. Stay away from my family, or you're going to have something a lot more serious to deal with than a prison sentence. Understand?"

Her eyes narrowed at him. "Are you threatening me?"

He just shrugged and knocked on the door, indicating they were done. "You heard what I said. Let's go girls."

Drew opened the door for them and as they filed out, Gabrielle called after them. "Abby! Noel! Wait!"

Neither sister turned to acknowledge her. They just filed out of the small room, went to the front desk, and turned in the signed restraining order paperwork.

Noel took a few moments to say her goodbyes to Drew, and then the three of them got into Abby's SUV.

"Are you two okay?" Lincoln asked.

Abby gripped the steering wheel, taking deep breaths, trying to calm herself as her stomach started to turn again.

"I'm perfect," Noel said from the back seat. "Honestly, I feel like a weight was lifted."

"Abby?" her father prompted.

She let out a long breath. "Yeah. I'm okay."

"Do you two have time for a short detour before you need to go your separate ways?" he asked, sounding a little self-conscious.

Abby turned to him. "Where are we going, Dad?"

"Just head down Main Street. It's just a couple of blocks."

"Okay, if you say so." Abby glanced in the rearview mirror, catching her sister's gaze. Noel made an I-have-no-idea face. Abby made one back to her and then did as her father asked.

A minute later, he said, "Stop here."

Abby craned her neck to read the sign for Enchanted Jewelers. "What are we getting here? Please don't tell me you want to get a new crystal, because I gotta tell you, I'm so over those."

"No. This is something else." He climbed out and held the door open for Noel while Abby hurried over to them.

"Okay, Dad. You have our attention. What is it?" Abby demanded.

He just walked into the jeweler without answering and greeted the pretty brunette behind the counter. "Syd, these are two of my daughters, Abby and Noel."

"Nice to meet you," the lady, whom Abby judged to be in her late forties, said as she shook their hands.

Abby briefly wondered if there was something going on between them but quickly dismissed it when Lincoln asked, "Is the ring ready?"

"Ring?" Noel parroted. "You purchased a ring? An *engagement* ring?"

Abby clutched her sister's arm, waiting for her father's reply.

Syd handed Lincoln a small blue-velvet box.

"Thanks," he said and opened it as he turned to his daughters. "Do you think Clair will like it?"

Abby's eyes filled with tears as she took in the beautiful diamond ring that was surrounded by black onyx. It was elegant and not too traditional, exactly like Clair. "It's perfect, Dad. Absolutely perfect."

"She's right," Noel added, beaming at her father. "Clair is going to love this."

He nodded at them and handed over his credit card.

Moments later, they were back in the SUV, headed to the Townsend family home. When Abby parked out front, Lincoln didn't get out of the car.

"I was going to ask her last month," he said quietly. "But then…" He sucked in a breath. "I had some questionable test results."

"What?" Abby's heart nearly beat right out of her chest. Her dad had battled cancer not that long ago and had been in remission. If it had come back… She blinked back fresh tears, trying to hold it together for whatever he had to say.

"Dad? What tests?" Noel prompted.

"My blood work was off, and Gerry wanted scans," he said. "I finally got everything back last week and I'm fine. So stop worrying about that," he added after he studied their expressions. "I'm only telling you this because it's why I didn't take Clair to the coast. It wasn't fair to ask her if I was going to have to go through treatments again."

Abby gaped at him. "Are you kidding?"

"Dad!" Noel admonished. "Clair wouldn't leave you if your cancer came back. That's crazy talk."

"I know," he said, sounding exasperated. "But I couldn't ask her to marry me with that hanging over our heads. I just… needed to wait until I knew."

They were both silent as they took that in. Finally Abby sucked in a breath and said, "Okay. Now you know. And you're going to ask her, when?"

"On the Solstice, out on the coast. I'm telling you two because I'm going to go in there and ask her to pack a bag, and then we're leaving for a few days. I don't want anyone to worry, and Abby, she won't be available to watch Lynette. Can you work with that?"

Abby grinned. "I can so work with that." She reached across the SUV and grabbed her father in a big hug. Noel reached over the seat, joining them. When they finally let go, Abby nodded to the door. "Go on. Go get her, Dad. You've kept us all waiting for far too long."

He gave her a rueful smile. "I guess you're right. Wish me luck."

"Luck!" his daughters said in unison.

When he disappeared inside, Noel quickly got into the front seat and said, "Go. Let's get out of here. I think I need a drink."

Abby laughed and took off down the long tree-lined driveway. Just as she was pulling out to head back into town, her phone buzzed. "Noel, can you get that?"

"Sure thing, little sis." Noel tapped the phone. "Hello... no, this is Noel, her sister." She pulled the phone away from her ear. "They have test results for you."

Abby pressed a button on her dash so that the call switched to Bluetooth. "Gerry? It's Abby. You have my results?"

"I do," the healer said, sounding far too pleased with herself.

"Let me guess, I don't have anything. The tests were clear," Abby said.

"Yes... and no," Gerry said. "You definitely don't have a virus."

"Okay. That's good considering we just found out my mother cursed me and that's what was making me sick."

"Hmm, maybe. Or maybe that's why my magical scan was inconclusive and I didn't catch this last week," Gerry mused.

"What? What are you talking about?" Abby asked. "Did you find something else?"

"Not a what, Abby. A who. You're pregnant."

Noel's eyes went wide as saucers as her mouth dropped open.

Abby immediately pulled the SUV over and continued to grip the steering wheel just to have something to hang onto. "Say that again? You think I'm pregnant?"

"I don't think you are, Abby. I know you are. I'm staring at the blood test results right now. If you want to come in again—"

"Oh my gods!" Abby cried. "I'm pregnant!" Joy filled every part of her being. "That's... oh my gosh. I can hardly believe it."

"I wanted to call and let you know as soon as

possible. Call me back for a follow up appointment once the shock wears off, okay?"

"Okay," Abby said and ended the call. She turned to her sister and said. "I'm pregnant."

"I heard," Noel said with a laugh. "I guess this is good news?"

"It's fantastic news. Clay is going to lose his mind."

"Then you better get moving," Noel said. "I don't want to be the only one whose had their mind blown today."

Abby giggled and put the SUV in gear. She had some very good news to deliver.

CHAPTER 13

*a*fter Abby dropped Noel off, she stopped at Incantation Café for pastries and hot chocolate. Her girls were at home and after she told Clay her news, she wanted to celebrate with them too.

"Abby," Hanna said when she got to the counter. "You're absolutely glowing today."

"I am?" Abby asked, feeling a little self-conscious. She didn't want to tell anyone else about her pregnancy until she was able to tell Clay.

"Yeah. Are you using a new facial cleanser or something?"

Abby laughed. "Not unless you count dog slobber."

Hanna gave her a quick once over. "You know, if it made me glow like that, I'd use it."

"You don't need any special cleanser. You're already beautiful," Abby reassured her friend.

Hanna rolled her eyes, but there was a pleased smile on her face. "Go take a seat. I'll have these ready for you in just a second."

"I'm going to sit at a table outside, okay? It's really nice out there," Abby said.

"Got it. See you in a few."

Abby exited the busy café and sat at the table farthest away from the front door. The sun was out, and it was unusually warm for early spring in their area. She took her sweater off and draped it over the back of her seat. When she turned back around, she nearly fell out of her chair when she spotted Charlotte's ghost sitting across from her.

"Charlotte?" she whispered, almost afraid to scare her friend away.

Abby, her friend said with a kind smile.

"How are you here"?" Abby asked her earnestly.

Just for a visit. Now that you're safe, I can go again. Her friend started to rise from the chair, but Abby reached her hand out, trying to stop her. It was fruitless of course, since Charlotte was a ghost. But it did make her pause.

"Will I see you again?" Abby asked, sounding kind of desperate even to her own ears.

Time will tell. I love you, Abs.

Abby wanted to scream, to try to make her stay. She wanted more time with her. Just a few words weren't enough. But her friend had already faded away into the ether.

The door to the café opened, and Hanna strolled out with Abby's order. She was just about to put everything down on the table when she stiffened. "Charlotte?"

"Do you see her?" Abby asked, breathless.

"I *feel* her," Hanna clarified. "She's here. I just know it. Charlotte?"

I'm here, Hanna, Charlotte said.

Hanna's big brown eyes filled with unshed tears. "Can I see you?"

There was a slight flicker of light and then Charlotte was there again, standing right in front of her sister.

Hanna let out a small gasp and reached for her but had the same problem Abby had. There was no touching a ghost.

Charlotte's smile was bittersweet as she stared at her sister. *Gorgeous. I'm proud of you, sis. Very proud.*

The flicker happened again, and when Charlotte vanished, Abby instinctively knew she was really gone this time.

Hanna slid into the empty chair, her hand clutching at her heart. "Did that really happen, or did I dream it?"

"It really happened," Abby said automatically.

Her friend eyed her suspiciously. "Is that the first time you've seen her?"

Abby shook her head.

"Tell me," Hanna said, leaning forward on her elbows.

Swallowing hard, Abby said, "She came earlier this week and warned me that I was in danger."

"She did?""

"Yes. I was going to tell you about it, but…" Abby waved her hand around. "Everything sort of blew up, and then I didn't want your feelings to be hurt, and I don't know, I just… Maybe I didn't handle it right."

"Abby!" Hanna said, covering her hand. "What are you talking about? My sister, your best friend, came to warn you about a bad actor. Do you know how huge that is? I just hope that if anyone curses me, she'll make sure I know. But she is my big sister. She might just think I deserve a comeuppance."

Abby laughed. "She wouldn't do that to you."

"No? Want me to tell you about the time she flushed my Barbie because my silence annoyed her? Yes, my silence. Now tell me that isn't a sister who is willing to throw me under the bus."

"Okay, you might have a point, but did you hear her? She's proud of you." Abby smiled. "And so am I. You're incredible."

"Stop," Hanna said with mock modesty. "You're embarrassing me."

Abby got to her feet and pulled her friend up too. Then she hugged her, holding on for as long as Hanna would let her. "I'm glad Charlotte showed up for you. You deserved that visit."

When Hanna pulled back, she wiped her eyes and said, "Yeah, I did, didn't I?"

"No doubt," she agreed.

The two talked for a few more minutes until Hanna had to go back to work. But before she did, she said, "You know, I don't think it's soap or dog slobber. You're pregnant, aren't you?"

The accusation was so out of the blue that it made Abby do a double take. "What? Why are you saying that?"

She grinned. "Charlotte just told me." Then Hanna winked and disappeared back into the café.

ABBY WALKED INTO HER HOUSE, a secret smile claiming her lips.

Olive immediately looked up from the phone in her hand and eyed the pastry bag. "Is that for us?"

"It sure is." Abby handed the bag to her stepdaughter

and then placed the drinks on the coffee table. "There's a hot chocolate for you and one for Lynette. Can you help her so that she doesn't spill it while I go talk to your dad?"

"Hot chocolate, too!" Olive's face lit up with pleasure. "Absolutely." She grabbed one of the cups and turned to Lynnette, who was already reaching for it. "Hold it with two hands," she coached the toddler.

Abby's heart melted as she watched them, but when she spotted her husband just outside on the patio, she moved toward him like there was some sort of gravitational pull.

She opened the door and quietly slipped out. He didn't seem to hear her as she walked up behind him and wrapped her arms around his torso, plastering herself to his back.

"Hey," he said softly, covering her hands with his as he turned his head back and gave her a quick kiss on the cheek. "How did it go?"

"As awful as you'd expect. But after we left, things got decidedly better," she said.

He turned in her arms and cupped her cheek with his good hand. "Is that so? What happened?"

She grinned up at him. "Dad bought a ring. He's taking Clair to the coast to ask her to marry him."

"You're kidding," he said with a shake of his head. "I thought I'd never see the day."

"Honestly, I didn't think so either. But he picked out

a gorgeous ring that is perfect for her and said he's taking her today, so I think it's actually happening now."

"I'll be damned. It's about time." He craned his head, looking past her toward the house. "That's not the only good news of the day."

"Oh?" Abby asked, suddenly wondering if Gerry had called him, too.

"Olive has a date tomorrow," he said, sounding like a proud papa. But then his tone shifted to an overprotective papa bear when he added, "With some fifteen-year-old punk who was too chicken to ask her out first."

Abby laughed. "So she took your advice then?"

"She did. I told her that if she liked him, she should just see if he wanted to hang out some time. And she did. It turns out he's been wanting to ask her out for a while now, but didn't know how to do it."

"Maybe he just doesn't have an awesome dad like you to guide him," she said, running her hands up his arms and clasping them around his neck.

"I'm sure that's it," he agreed with a laugh.

"Where are they going, anyway?" Abby asked him.

"Ice skating over at the Pelsh winery. It's the last skate of the season, and her cousin Daisy is going too, so Noel said she'd drive them."

"Tomorrow?" Abby pressed.

"Yeah, why?"

"We're going to need to ask your mother to watch Lynette." Abby ran one hand up to bury it into his hair.

His eyebrows rose as he studied her. "Why is that, Mrs. Garrison? Do you have plans for me?"

"Yes. We're celebrating." She pressed up onto her tiptoes and gave him a slow, but very thorough kiss. When she pulled away, he tried to chase her lips, but she put one finger up against his mouth, stopping him. "Don't you want to know what we're celebrating?"

"Being alone?" he asked hopefully.

She chuckled. "Not quite." Abby took a small step back and ran one hand down her torso until it was plastered against her lower abdomen. "It turns out that we won't actually be completely alone."

His eyes followed, and she knew the moment her news registered. "Abs? Are you saying what I think you're saying?"

She nodded, her eyes filling with tears. "Yes. Gerry called. The curse was masking it. I know we weren't trying, but the blood test confirmed it. We're having a baby."

Clay stared down at her with so much love in his eyes that Abby's heart nearly melted. Then he pulled her back into his arms and whispered, "You're incredible. You know that?"

"You're the one who got me this way," she said with a giggle.

"Hmm, that's true." He nuzzled her neck. "Do you think we can get rid of the kids right now?"

"Why? You can't wait until tomorrow?" she asked breathlessly.

"Ew, get a room!" Olive said from the back door.

Clay lifted his head to look at his daughter. "Was there something you needed, Olive?"

"Yeah. Lynette is covered in pumpkin pastry and Endora's slobber. She needs a bath, ASAP."

"Duty calls," Abby said with a chuckle.

Clay sighed and then gave her a secret smile. "Tomorrow it is then."

"Tomorrow," she agreed, and then they walked hand in hand back into the house, both of them filled with joy.

DEANNA'S BOOK LIST

Witches of Keating Hollow:
Soul of the Witch
Heart of the Witch
Spirit of the Witch
Dreams of the Witch
Courage of the Witch
Love of the Witch
Power of the Witch
Essence of the Witch
Muse of the Witch
Vision of the Witch
Waking of the Witch
Honor of the Witch
Promise of the Witch
Gift of the Witch

Return of the Witch

Fortune of the Witch

Keating Hollow Happily Ever Afters:

Gift of the Witch

Wisdom of the Witch

Witches of Befana Bay:

The Witch's Silver Lining

Witches of Christmas Grove:

A Witch For Mr. Holiday

A Witch For Mr. Christmas

A Witch For Mr. Winter

A Witch For Mr. Mistletoe

A Witch For Mr. Frost

Premonition Pointe Novels:

Witching For Grace

Witching For Hope

Witching For Joy

Witching For Clarity

Witching For Moxie

Witching For Kismet

Miss Matched Midlife Dating Agency:

Star-crossed Witch

Honor-bound Witch
Outmatched Witch
Moonstruck Witch

Jade Calhoun Novels:
Haunted on Bourbon Street
Witches of Bourbon Street
Demons of Bourbon Street
Angels of Bourbon Street
Shadows of Bourbon Street
Incubus of Bourbon Street
Bewitched on Bourbon Street
Hexed on Bourbon Street
Dragons of Bourbon Street

Pyper Rayne Novels:
Spirits, Stilettos, and a Silver Bustier
Spirits, Rock Stars, and a Midnight Chocolate Bar
Spirits, Beignets, and a Bayou Biker Gang
Spirits, Diamonds, and a Drive-thru Daiquiri Stand
Spirits, Spells, and Wedding Bells

Ida May Chronicles:
Witched To Death
Witch, Please
Stop Your Witchin'

Crescent City Fae Novels:
Influential Magic

Irresistible Magic

Intoxicating Magic

Last Witch Standing:
Bewitched by Moonlight

Soulless at Sunset

Bloodlust By Midnight

Bitten At Daybreak

Witch Island Brides:
The Wolf's New Year Bride

The Vampire's Last Dance

The Warlock's Enchanted Kiss

The Shifter's First Bite

Destiny Novels:
Defining Destiny

Accepting Fate

Wolves of the Rising Sun:
Jace

Aiden

Luc

Craved

Silas

Darien

Wren

Black Bear Outlaws:

Cyrus

Chase

Cole

Bayou Springs Alien Mail Order Brides:

Zeke

Gunn

Echo

ABOUT THE AUTHOR

New York Times and USA Today bestselling author, Deanna Chase, is a native Californian, transplanted to the slower paced lifestyle of southeastern Louisiana. When she isn't writing, she is often goofing off with her husband in New Orleans or playing with her two shih tzu dogs. For more information and updates on newest releases visit her website at deannachase.com.

www.ingramcontent.com/pod-product-compliance
Lightning Source LLC
Chambersburg PA
CBHW051958170626
46808CB00007B/2679